# A TOMB IN THE ROCKS

If you enjoy this book, please leave a review. It helps other people discover Alex's books. You can sign up for the newsletter to get updates on future books.

**AlexGuyBooks.com**

McSteed Inc / Chris Neuhahn

Cover Design by Chris Neuhahn
ChrisNeuhahn.com

1st edition 2024

ISBN 978-1-963090-00-0
ISBN 978-1-963090-01-7 (ebook)

# A TOMB IN THE ROCKS

## ALEXANDER GUY

For the Rabbit, who puts up with me chasing whims.

And for those who risk it all.

*For my part, whatever anguish of spirit it may cost, I am willing to know the whole truth; to know the worst and provide for it.*

—Patrick Henry

# CHAPTER ONE

J oey threw himself face down in the crater, grunting from the impact, and wedged his gloved hands between the abrasive soil and his glass helmet, protecting it. He wasn't scared. Not exactly. His heart pounded with excitement, not fear. The coming rogue asteroid wasn't yet real in his mind.

"Rock! Rock! Rock!" Foreman Kalil shouted again, his voice tinny in the speakers of Joey's pressure suit. "Everyone down!"

Nearly one hundred miners had dropped and lay prone, scattered around the half-kilometer-wide crater. They had drilled for this many times. The older miners had even been through the real thing. But this was Joey's first. He was twelve, and the wait was boring.

He spread his fingers, peering through them to the regolith, studying the gritty soil. Sunlight glittered off the tiny facets, a subtle beauty in the gray. He pushed his face and the dome of his helmet as close as he dared. Even a small scratch could weaken it. And in the vacuum of space, you must take care of your equipment. Olly didn't take care of his equipment and it cost him dearly. Everything Olly did cost him dearly. *Don't be an Olly*, Joey chided himself, and lifted the fused-quartz dome to a safer distance.

The entertainment in the regolith ran its course. Joey arched his back and looked around, craning his neck. There was a large rock jutting from the ground to his left. He pulled himself to the rock and pressed his back against it, getting as close as the bulk of his Angel pressure suit would let him. He checked the front of the suit for damage. Nothing. He was an Oscar there.

From his upright position he watched the miners start to fidget. It seemed they were getting bored too. Some dared to raise themselves to see if the rogue asteroid was near. But it wasn't.

And the waiting dragged on.

Around the rim of the crater, twenty foremen knelt on one knee. They were statues except for their heads, which were on a swivel. The foremen were easy to spot with the red band running down the leg of their Angel. They faced out from the dig site as they always did, their rifles slung in front of their chests where they could be whipped up in a flash. While everyone sheltered, they stood watch in case reffies came.

Joey pulled out his spiral-bound notebook and stainless steel–barreled grease pencil. He flipped open the book, flipped past stiff plasticized pages filled with drawings of equipment and notes on their operation. Joey had no idea what other miners had in their notebooks. Asking them might have led to them asking to see what was in his, and the inside of his notebook was decidedly Olly.

Once he found a blank page, he hesitated and looked around. No one paid him any attention. He sketched, light at first to get the overall form, then he worked on the details.

He drew the miners in the distance. None were near enough to him, so he invented a miner lying closer because he wanted to see the expression on his face in the drawing. From his comic books he'd recently learned a simple way to draw eyes and expressions. The fear was visible in only a handful of well-placed lines. He stared at the face and the fear became real for him. But he kept drawing, distracting himself.

Joey became lost in the drawing. He spent extra time shading and adjusting. He had captured the moment. The bravery of the foreman. The fear of the miners. It was all there, captured in a way he never had before. A satisfied smile spread across his face. In the corner of the drawing he wrote, "First Rogue Asteroid! June 13, 2171."

Inside the ring joint at the base of his helmet, the red warning light came on and flashed in slow, steady pulses.

"Seven-meter rock," Foreman Kalil said. "Lots of Trojans."

In school, Joey had learned about Trojans, the trails of smaller rocks pulled along in the gravitational wake of an asteroid. They could be more dangerous, more deadly. Sweat dribbled from Joey's messy hair, landing in the moisture collector at the base of the helmet.

The red light pulsed in twos now. Blink, blink. Blink, blink.

This was not like the drills. Not even close. His fingers trembled.

The red light blinked in threes now.

"Here it comes," Foreman Kalil shouted.

Now it blinked in fours. In fives. A rapid, impatient flashing.

Joey pressed himself tighter against the rock. Seven meters was not a large asteroid. Three times the height of a man. But there was no missing the oblong gray mass. It was plenty big to grind miner and foreman into a paste along the ground. But it glided silently some twenty meters above their heads. The shadow it cast over the men and boys in the crater was absolute, blacker than the star-filled sky.

*We could have kept working,* Joey thought. He chuckled to himself. Joseph Senior would have liked that line of thinking from his son. Maybe he'd even brag about it to his dad tonight.

Joey added the shadow of the asteroid to the drawing, fighting to keep his hand steady.

A memory surfaced. From when Joey was young. From well before he started the six years of mining school. Perhaps his earliest memory—his young mind could not tell what was real from the gaps his imagination filled. He had seen lights on an asteroid drifting overhead. Blue lights. He'd been told it was an illusion, a play of sunlight on minerals in the asteroid. He'd seen faint blue sparkles in the soil before, so that idea made sense to him now.

As the rogue asteroid receded into the black of space, the red light slowed to two flashes again. And then to one.

Joey hadn't realized his every muscle had been clenched until he let them go slack. He stood. The break in the day was nice, and he couldn't wait for the next one.

The red light blinked in fives again.

"Joey, get back down! ROCKS! ROCKS! ROCKS!" yelled Foreman Alejo. The foreman, who had been far closer than Joey realized, jumped down from the rim of the crater and threw himself to the ground a few meters from Joey.

"Trojans incoming," Alejo said, his eyes pleading with Joey to get down.

Joey dropped to the protective rock again, nearly hitting his glass dome. He cursed himself. The rest of the foremen jumped into the crater, pressing themselves to the ground. Joey was the only one not lying flat, but he was too scared to move.

In the field of miners, someone stood.

Then the Trojans came and nothing else mattered. All around him was violence. Thousands of small rocks ripped past, a lethal sideways rain. Rocks streaked overhead, and to his left and right, and they skipped along the ground. They exploded against the crater wall, and against the rock where Joey sheltered. The ground shuddered as if the asteroid beneath him was tearing apart.

Joey pulled his legs in tight. His panting fogged the glass in front of his face. He scrunched his eyes until they hurt. He gritted his teeth until he tasted blood.

A piercing electronic wail erupted from the speaker in Joey's suit, and then a scream. It was a scream of death that cut short almost as soon as it started.

But it reverberated in his helmet, and he cried at the horror of it.

Shouts of pain and fear broke through ShortComs as the squall of rocks went on.

"Dad?" Joey said. His voice broke.

"Keep the line clear," snapped Foreman Ganyon.

Joey cursed himself. None of the other boys called out for their dads. None of the other boys got Ganyon's attention. If they were crying like he was, they kept it hidden.

"I'm still here, Joey."

"Keep it clear, damn it."

# CHAPTER TWO

J oey shuffled with the crowd up the wide metal ramp at the far edge of the crater. The ramp rattled with the chaotic rhythm of dozens of Angel boots and reverberated through his soles. But the racket could not drown out the death scream still echoing in Joey's ears.

He snapped his pickaxe, shovel, and debris brush into their metal clips on the equipment rack. Like the ore processors and AGLS recharge stations, the racks had escaped the fury of the Trojans. The equipment only suffered dents and easily patched holes. Most of the rocks hit the crater and beyond. Out there, an outpost foreman station had been destroyed, along with a pair of one-seat rock runners and their refuel pumps.

Before the end of the shift, Joey had learned his dad's friend had been killed, a quiet but respected miner named Felix. It was Felix's scream that lingered in Joey's ears. Rocks had punched through his head and body and threw his remains a kilometer away. Joey had spoken to him a few times, but the man never said much. That he was gone now was distant, too hard to grasp. But the scream was not distant.

"Joey."

A hand grabbed Joey's shoulder. The boy turned to find Foreman Alejo smiling at him.

"I saw what you were drawing, kid," Alejo said.

Joey's breath caught in his throat. Smile or no, he didn't imagine drawing on the job was okay.

"It was really good," Alejo said.

"Oh," Joey said, relieved. "Thank you, sir."

"But keep it to breaks, okay? Don't want people calling you Olly."

"No, sir. I'm no Olly." Joey smiled.

"Alright. Have a good night, Joey. Tell your dad hello."

"Thank you, sir. I will."

People saw him drawing. That meant his dad might know. Imagining his dad lecturing him tonight stole his smile.

Joey rejoined the stream of miners leaving the dig site. When they were close enough, scraps of conversations carried over ShortComs. It was mostly banter about dinner or friendly jabs about who was more scared of the rogue rock. The asteroid was bigger than the last one. No, it was smaller than the last one. Those were nothing compared to some other year.

They complained about damage to their suits. Rocks had punctured life support packs, the suit's woven PTFE shells, and shattered dust-repellant systems. There would be many repairs tonight, and some outright replacements. But The Mining Society always had more. Miners were never charged for repairs. Unless negligence was suspected. But shame kept that problem at bay.

One miner suffered a freeze burn when a pea-sized rock tore his pant leg. Another miner had slapped on an emergency patch before the exposure could kill the flesh and before he ran out of air. But it still meant a trip to the infirmary, and a loss of satisfaction for the day's work. A boy took a rock to the arm, snapping the bones. Even with bone healer, he'd be out a few days.

Joey saw Benjamin Junior, one of the other young miners, walking with his dad.

"Hey, Ben."

"Hey, Joey," Ben said without enthusiasm.

"Did you hear about Felix?"

"Yeah. Dad said it was his fault."

Benjamin Senior scoffed.

"It was. His stinkin' dome broke on account of he didn't take care of the glass. Foreman Aceveda seen the pitting himself. Been there two days at least, Aceveda said."

Joey had seen Felix that morning. He didn't remember any pitting, but he supposed it could have been there.

"I believe it," someone else said. "These domes can take a hell of a hit."

*Hell of a hit?* Joey remembered the violence of the Trojans.

"Yeah, old Paul took a pickaxe to his 'cause some dope weren't paying attention. Had to be replaced, but it didn't bust. Paul is an Oscar with his equipment like nobody. Saved his damn life."

"Yep," Benjamin Senior said. "Felix was an Olly.

No question about that."

"Don't know, seemed like a hard worker to me," Joey said. Someone being an "Olly" was the catchall term for bad behavior. So much for Felix being respected. His years of contribution were wiped away. Oscar to Olly in a storm of rocks. But Joey had seen someone stand right before the Trojans came. No one mentioned that. Had it been Felix? It must have. He couldn't have been the only one to see. Why someone would stand with the Trojans coming, he didn't know. Of course, Joey had stood on accident. Maybe Felix had too.

"One Olly defending another," Ben Junior said.

Laughter broke out around Joey. He frowned.

"I'm not an Olly," Joey snapped.

The laughter erupted again, and Joey walked faster to get away from the other miners.

It was eight hundred and fifty-three steps to the miners' village. He frequently counted his steps, and other routine tasks, to drown out the distractions. He counted now with vigor.

Floating in his head with the stream of numbers, and the steady crunch of his steps, was the scream. *Maybe they were right. Felix didn't take care of his equipment. I take care of my equipment,* Joey thought. *I am not an Olly. Felix was.*

The idea of Felix as an Olly was easier to understand than the idea that he stood. There were no stories about Olly standing.

# CHAPTER THREE

The Mining Society, or TMS, spared no expense on equipment. Bad equipment led to bad morale, and TMS prided itself on the quality of life for its citizens. Their model was an inspiration for new colonies all around the solar system.

Decent food and comfortable pressure suits were the first keys to morale. Citizens spent long hours in their suits, so they had to be perfect in every way. The Mark IV Artificial Gravity Life Support suit, or Angel, had dozens of micro thrusters to simulate Earth's gravity accurately for each part of the body, and they pulled toward the ground no matter how the miner was angled. Most miners would retire to Earth or Mars someday, and the suit ensured they had the bone density. The shell was threaded with charged carbon filaments that repelled the asteroid dust. Keeping the destructive dust out of living spaces was another key to morale. Once the dust was inside, it got into everything, from electronics to eyeballs, and irritated it all.

As comfortable as the Mark IV was, Joey could

not wait to get to his apartment and get out of it. His dad would be making dinner soon and Joey's stomach growled at the thought.

At step three hundred and thirty-seven, Joey walked under the shadow of the central control tower. Nicknamed the Mushroom, it was a large white dome encircled by panoramic windows. The dome sat atop a ten-meter central column so it could overlook all mining operations.

The crowd weaved around the dozens of cables that anchored the top-heavy building to the surface. Like most structures on the asteroid, the Mushroom's shape balanced function with transportability. The odd shapes interlocked with other equipment, and within the lattice framework of the asteroid-to-asteroid transports.

As the crowd left the shadow of the Mushroom, they dispersed. Some people went off to the commissary, others who didn't have kitchens in their apartments, or lived in the bunkhouses, headed to the mess hall.

"Joey," Stan called out. Twenty-six steps earlier than normal. Joey smiled. Besides Joseph Senior, Stan was his only friend. Stan closed the oval hatch at the base of the Mushroom, pulled the latch tight and jogged over.

"Hey, Stan. How was classes today?"

"How *were* classes today," Stan corrected.

"What?"

"Oh, never mind."

Stanford Emerson VII was fourteen years old, the only boy in the colony who wasn't either twelve or eighteen. He would be a foreman in a few years, and likely elected governor when his dad retired. Legally, any foreman could be elected governor, but everyone voted for an Emerson.

"Classes were boring," Stan said, "as per the schedule."

"Come on. What'd you learn?"

Stan sighed.

"Boring stuff about sensors for ore processing. And some pricing tables for ore markets. The only thing that was even slightly interesting was stellar cartography and spectral classifications."

"What?" Joey asked. Joey rarely understood everything Stan said. So many of the words were foreign.

"Charting the locations of asteroids, and the rating of the color and reflectivity of the same. But truly, that was boring too. So I know the location of another gray rock."

"You rate the colors of the rock?" Joey said.

"The sensors do. They calculate how boring the gray is."

"It ain't as boring as it looks."

"So the sensors keep telling me."

Joey laughed.

"It sounds neat to me," Joey said, "I mean, what I can follow. I like when you tell me about it."

"I have to. The way I see it, that's why teachers teach. So they aren't left holding on to all that concentrated boredom."

"Oh," Joey said. He smiled. Joey liked the way Stan talked. None of the miners spoke like him. Joey tried to talk like Stan with the other twelve year olds. It went over like a pickaxe to the foot.

"You had some excitement today," Stan said, perking up.

"Excitement?" Joey said. "I felt the rocks hitting the ground. Even the little ones. Like how the impact drills shake everything. It was scary."

"We had to evacuate the tower." Stan sounded disappointed. "We stayed in the bunker pit for the whole thing. It would have been a nice break, but the tutor kept at it. I would have rather been out in the crater with you."

"It wasn't fun," Joey said. *But it was kind of exciting,* he admitted to himself. At least until the small rocks came. If Stan knew about Felix or the other injuries, he didn't seem affected by it. Joey didn't want to talk about it, so maybe it was better that way.

"It sounds stimulating, at least," Stan said.

"Yeah. I guess," Joey said sourly.

Governor Stanford Emerson VI stepped out of the Mushroom. His AGLS was pristine and had golden-yellow bands where the foremen's had red. He strode over to the two boys. Everything about the man was smooth: his purposeful walk, his whisker-free chin, his hair. Dark and streaked with gray, his hair reminded Joey of molded plastic. The governor gave Joey a brief smile, then turned his attention to his son.

"Stanford," the governor said. Even his voice was smooth. "You'll be expected at the evening meal."

"Yes, Father," Stan said. "I hoped we could talk at dinner."

"I'm busy. Is it important?"

Stan shrugged.

"I thought I could tell you about my studies."

All the older boy's disdain for his studies seemed to vanish.

"Son," the governor said, "I know your studies. I wrote the curriculum and, indeed, many of the lessons myself. Was there anything else?"

Stan deflated.

"No, Father. See you later, Joey."

"See you," Joey said.

"Tell your father hello for me, Joseph Junior," the governor said with a smile, and he led his son away.

"Yes, Governor."

After Stan and the governor climbed back into the Mushroom, Joey headed for the village.

# CHAPTER FOUR

Joey neared the first street of the village. The street for miners with sons. Farther along the main path were streets of one-room apartments, and beyond that were the six-to-a-room bunkhouses. The crowd had thinned to just a few others.

The apartments were boxes, three meters tall and ten meters along the side. Each box had a large oval window and a heavy airlock hatch facing the street. At the corners were attachment points for transportation. Every other surface was wrapped in a dozen insulating layers of crinkled white Mylar and hex mesh.

Joey turned down his street, and when he was sure no one watched, he played. He jumped over the shadows of the anchor straps that stretched from box to box across the path overhead. Each narrow shadow was a massive chasm that could only be jumped by the bravest of men. When he was tall enough, he would swing from the straps. For now he was content to pretend.

As he approached his apartment, the last in the

row, he decided he would not discuss the death of Felix unless his dad did.

He swung the outer airlock door open. Felt the grit in the hinges. They would have to be cleaned soon. He stepped through the hatch and pulled the door closed.

Inside the cramped airlock vestibule, Joey punched the large green button with the base of his fist. The buttons took effort so they could not be engaged accidentally. As air flooded the small chamber, the muffled sounds of the apartment joined the claustrophobic reverb in the Angel suit. A blast of air buffeted him as it removed any remaining dust that clung to the shell.

The green button lit up, telling him it was safe to breathe inside. Joey vented his suit and worked his jaw to equalize the pressure in his ears. He removed his helmet, enjoying the unrestricted movement of his head and the symphony of sound. In the Angel he mostly heard his own breathing, the creaking of the suit's shell, and the knife slice of stainless-steel ring joints.

Step-by-step, Joey peeled himself out of the AGLS, releasing the dozens of straps that ensured each micro thruster group affected the right part of the body. Once the last strap was loose and he stepped out of the boots, he felt the freedom of RN-3a's low gravity.

After hanging the suit on the hook next to his dad's, he attached the ventilation hoses that would clean, dry, and freshen the interior. Seeing the two suits together gave him a swell of pride. It was his first cycle as a miner, and he was already exceeding quota, just like his old man.

Ben Junior and the others could call him Olly if they wanted. Just last week, they had looked at him like a slug in their food when he suggested they could beat quota if they dug based on the color of the rock rather than only the grid they were assigned.

"Look at Olly over here," Michael had said. "This first-cycle brat thinks he knows how to mine better than TMS. Kid, they been at this generations. I think they know what's what."

Joey mostly dug the grid now, and TMS saw his output. That's what mattered. Joey was sure his way was better, but maybe Michael was right. TMS probably had a good reason for the way they did it.

He grabbed his notebook and grease pencil from the holder on the hip of his Angel and put them in the back pocket of his undergarment. He grabbed the latch handle for the inner airlock door. On the other side of the window, Joseph Senior was already in his house clothes, snug but flexible quilted pants and a long-sleeve knit shirt, in a light cream color that showed any potential dust clearly. Joey smiled and yanked the latch to slide the door open.

The piercing door buzzer went off, then was silenced when he latched the door behind him. The buzzer sounded again. It was an awful sound that demanded attention. Joey pulled the handle hard until the solid clunk told him it was seated.

Joseph Senior was cooking dinner. Though he was a stocky man, dense with muscle, without the AGLS and in the low gravity, he was graceful as he prepared their meal.

"Hi, Dad," Joey said.

"Joey," Joseph Senior said. He was beaming. "Hurry and get showered. Food's almost ready."

"Okay," Joey said. He stepped into the washroom right off the entrance opposite the compact kitchen.

# CHAPTER FIVE

S howered and starving, Joey leaned against the wall near the airlock door. The apartment was tight but bigger than most. Joseph Senior's excellent service had earned that, and the privilege to be a father. The only decorations in the main room were an arrangement of overlapping squares in soothing colors on one wall. Wall-mounted planters on either side held bushy air ferns. More ferns hung on the other walls. Drawings torn from Joey's old notebooks were taped up everywhere.

Joseph Senior looked back over his shoulder.

"Because we both beat quota last week, they let me buy a special dessert." He turned a cellophane package over in his thick fingers and read the label. "Turnover, comma, Spiced Apple. From Earth-grown apples!"

"Everyone in my age group says Mars has the best fruit."

"No offense to you, son, but your age group is fresh outta marbles. Mars is a lousy copy of Mother Earth. And don't even get me started on Io." Joseph senior let out a snort. "Io? Please."

Joey smiled. He liked to get his dad going on Mars versus Earth. Of course, they had never been to either. Like Joey, his dad had been born to the asteroid-hopping life of a TMS miner. A life that was neither paradise nor hell. Paradise came in retirement.

"Mother Earth," Joseph Senior continued, "the place where Joseph Senior, Senior, Senior came from. It's called El Paso, Texas, and it sounds like heaven. I'll be retiring there. And now that the idea is in my head. I can't wait to bite into a fresh apple."

"I don't want you to retire," Joey said.

"That's years from now, Joey," Joseph Senior said as he tore open a spice packet and poured it into the pot. "Your friends will be more important to you. Hell, you'll be old enough to have your own son."

Friends? Who would he be friends with? Ben Junior? Stan? He would be governor by then. Joey doubted he'd be sitting at the commissary bar listening to the governor complain about pricing tables.

"Now," Joseph Senior said with a sudden enthusiasm, "I know I always say pride in your work is its own reward."

Joey smiled and rolled his eyes. "You do always say that."

His dad always used quotes from *The Mining Society's Guide for Good Citizens* as if they were his own. Known simply as The Book, it was a collection of stories about Oscar and Oliver doing various tasks around the colony. Everything Oscar did worked out for the best because he followed the rules. Everything Oliver did cost him dearly.

"I do. On account of it being true," Joseph Senior said. "Wait. Listen."

Joey's dad paused. He cocked his head.

"We got a leak. Do you hear it?"

"Yeah," Joey said.

He moved away from the wall to look for the leak, and the Door Ajar buzzer pierced the air. Joey had been leaning on the buzzer next to the door. Joseph Senior laughed. He darted over to the airlock door and gave the handle a sharp tug. The buzzer shut off.

"That latch. I tell you...Oh, the food!"

Joseph Senior got back to the stove. Where Joey had drawing, his dad had cooking. The meals were prepackaged kits, but Joseph Senior always mixed ingredients from the different kits. Tomorrow's meat with today's spices. Friday's veggies with Monday's sauce.

Joseph Senior scooped a chicken thigh out of the pot for each of their food trays. He then poured a thick liquid from the smaller pot over the top. He slid two trays onto the wall-mounted table.

"Anyway, pride in your work is nice, but sometimes the reward is dessert. And that's nice too."

Joey smiled. "Yeah, that is nice."

"Right?! But first. Rosemary chicken thighs—whatever rosemary is—and that sticky sauce from the Thursday noodles. Plus, according to payday tradition, we got butter and that crusty bread you love. We eat like Earthlings tonight. Or Martians, I guess."

Joseph rustled Joey's hair and sat down.

"And I bought you a new comic book. It's on the counter over there."

Joey started to get up for the comic.

"Uh-uh," Joseph Senior said, "after dinner, bub."

Joseph Senior smiled warmly and Joey sat back down.

The chicken was delicious. The occasional special dessert was good, but his dad's cooking experiments, and eating with him, were the best part of every day.

All through dinner Joey and Joseph Senior talked and laughed. Joseph told a story about a rogue rock from many years ago. It had been bigger than the rock from today, and it hit the ground, taking out the stacks and a couple of foremen and a dozen miners, all of whom had failed to evacuate despite warnings. *I guess foremen are Ollys too.*

Joey wanted to ask if his dad knew any of them, but decided to avoid the subject in case it led to Felix's death.

The impact, even though it had been glancing, destabilized the main asteroid. The colony had been forced to relocate. A crew stayed back to mount stabilizing engines to the asteroid to keep it from falling out of orbit. There was too much valuable ore there to let it drift off, and to someday be swallowed by Jupiter.

After dinner and the spiced-apple dessert, Joey cleaned each pot. He dried them and put the damp towels into the moisture extractors. He was about to wipe the counters when his dad spoke.

"Why was Alejo talking at you," Joseph Senior asked.

Joey sagged. The evening was going so well.

"No reason. He told me to have a nice night," Joey said.

"I watched him walk straight for you and all he had to say was 'Have a nice night'?"

"Go figure." Joey could feel his dad's eyes on him. "Oh, he said to say hi to you."

"Joseph Junior. No point in hiding it from me."

Spanning generations, using a child's full birth name always said the same thing: start talking or pay the consequences.

Joey told him everything. He told him about the drawing and Alejo's compliment. He tried to show his dad the drawing, but Joseph Senior wasn't interested.

"When you're at the dig, what are you there to do?"

"He said he didn't mind," Joey protested.

"I mind. What are you there to do?"

"He liked my drawing."

"Junior."

"I'm there to dig," Joey said at last, "but nobody was digging on account of—"

"Ahh. You're there to dig, yes. We dig as our contribution to society. And we show our appreciation for all they give by doing our task well."

Joey suppressed a groan. More quotes from The Book.

"That's the agreement," Joseph Senior continued, "and we really should not stand out unless it's by doing our job well. Not by drawing."

"I thought you liked my drawings."

"I love your drawings. But you have the night for that."

Joseph handed him the comic book.

"I'll finish the kitchen," Joseph Senior said. "Go read your comic book."

Joey sighed. On the glossy cover was a drawing of Olly with a stupid smile as a piece of equipment was about to fall on him. No surprise. They were always Olly stories.

"It's just chapter three from The Book. I know that chapter by heart."

"Knowing the words ain't the same as knowing what it's all about," Joseph said with a smile.

"Yes, Dad."

# CHAPTER SIX

Joey turned sideways to squeeze between the bed and wall of his narrow room. He tossed the comic book into the cubbyhole set in the wall above his bed, then lay down. He gazed out the oval window opposite the door. At night the Milky Way usually shone brilliantly, but the Trojan storm had ejected a lot of dust. It could take months or even years for the cloud to settle back to the surface.

He watched for RN-3b, the moonlet asteroid to RN-3a. After a few minutes, it passed by, a mere crescent low on the horizon, beyond the white dome of the Mushroom.

Joey looked at his drawings, which covered the walls. He looked at his fingers. He looked at his knees. He looked at anything other the comic book. He wished for once he could read something that wasn't The Book, or based on The Book. He didn't disagree with The Book exactly. The stories of Olly and the dangers of not following the safety rules made sense. It was the other parts that bugged him. The depiction of Oscar, the good citizen. Those parts made it seem like chipping away at rock was a magical experience beyond the comprehension of man.

The way Joey saw it, his drawing were the opposite of Olly. He paid attention to all the little details just like Oscar. But his dad was right. Drawing itself wasn't Olly, but drawing when he was supposed to be mining was pure Olly.

In time, Joey picked up the comic book out of boredom. He only looked at the artwork. At least that was interesting. He wanted to know what they used to get the lines so clean and unbroken. With the grease pencil and the grainy marks it made, he could not replicate those lines. Joey liked the look of his drawings but wanted to do more.

There really was no reason to read the comic book. His eyes were hard to hold open now, and he truly did know the story by heart. And he knew exactly why his dad always had him read the same chapter, and got him this particular comic book, on this particular day.

In chapter three, section two of The Book, Olly was distracted by something that wasn't his job, and that caused an accident. In the comic books the situation changed each time. This time it was a four-seat rock runner that Olly was supposed to be tending. The heavy vehicle crushed Olly when it slid out of its harness. Last time it had been an Angel recharge pump explosion that did in the hapless miner and a dozen others. Olly frequently died. But never on purpose.

Not like Felix.

# CHAPTER SEVEN

Joey stepped out of the airlock and into the bright morning sun streaking through the ejecta. The dust clouds diffused the light and softened the usually stark shadows. With no atmosphere, whatever warmth he felt was from his Angel.

Joey wanted to draw the shafts of sunlight, but not today. Today he was determined to get his mind back on work. Not because The Book said so, or for TMS, but for his dad. He loved his dad, and he felt pride in being the son of someone so respected. He wanted to feel what his dad must feel. For that, he must absorb his dad's words: work is work and play is play.

He focused on the day of mining ahead, carving a place in his mind for other things. Drawing time was something to look forward to at the end of the day. After all, he still enjoyed his job despite the mindlessness of it, maybe even because of it. The meditative practice he had of counting the swings of his pickaxe made the day go by unnoticed sometimes. And he enjoyed the feeling in his body after a shift of being physically active. Even though he had only been mining for a few months, he could feel his strength growing and imagined the day when his fingers were thick like his dad's. They were hands of a respected miner.

"Joey," Joseph Senior called out.

Joey turned. His dad was exiting the airlock.

"Wait for me."

"Okay," Joey said.

His dad usually sent him ahead, wanting Joey to arrive to the dig "as his own man." This was an odd but welcome change. Welcome assuming they weren't going to rehash last night's conversation.

"We're only week until the next hop," Joseph Senior said. "It will be your first hop as a miner. It's always nice to mine a new rock after a while. And if they decide the crater is spent, we may get a couple extra days off."

"The crater is spent," Joey said. "Maybe another day."

"How do you know?" Joseph Senior said, looking like Joey had just told him he could fly.

Joey bit his tongue. Like a true chapter three Olly, Joey had watched the readout on the processing station display lower and lower yields. And the lower yields coincided with the crater having less of the dark gray rock with the faint blue sparkles.

Joey laughed to cover his panic. He didn't want to disappoint his dad. "I was joking. How the heck would I know?"

Joseph Senior gave him a curious smile and laughed.

## CHAPTER EIGHT

Joey and his dad joined the crowd walking from the miners' village to the crater. The jump to RN-1-2 was coming soon and spirits were up. Each cluster was mined in three-month cycles while they were in perihelion. Proximity to the sun ensured maximum power from the solar arrays, reducing the demand on hydrogen for the fuel cell generators. Transportation time was a week-long break from being in a pressure suit. And it was a week of eating freshly made food. Best of all, the bar served real alcohol. Even the strict cutoff after two drinks couldn't dampen that release.

"Joseph," a miner said, "think they'll call the dig early?"

"Don't know. Ask my son."

The miner looked at Joey.

"What? No," Joey panicked, "don't ask me."

The confused miner looked to Joseph for an explanation. Joseph laughed.

"Oh, I'm just having fun with Joey. Something we was talking about earlier."

"Right."

At the equipment racks, each miner grabbed their tools. When it was his turn, Joey grabbed his pickaxe, short-handled shovel, and hand brush. He checked for his initials on the handles as his dad had taught him. Each tool was owned by the individual miner but stored at the dig site. It cut down on the dust entering living spaces.

Joseph Senior grabbed his tools, racked next to Joey's. He frowned at the pickaxe and ran his gloved finger over the dull point.

"Time to retire this old fellow," he said. "Been sharpened too many times."

Joey held up his own pickaxe to compare. Despite being a youth's tool, it had a longer, sharper point.

"I have time now. See you tonight, Joey," Joseph Senior said and split out of the line.

"Bye, Dad," Joey said.

Joey stepped up to the middle line of the Angel recharge pump station. It was a box as tall as he was and had six hoses hanging from each insulation-wrapped side. The station extracted water from ice pockets deep below the surface. Some was separated into oxygen and hydrogen. Hydrogen powered the Angel's fuel cells, and the oxygen was mixed with nitrogen and added to the suit's air reserves. Water was stored in the Angel's backpack for both drinking and humidifying the air. And some of the hydrogen and oxygen were recombined into high-test peroxide for the micro thrusters.

Joey was soon near the front of the line. Beyond the pumps, the governor walked with Stan near the raised foreman overwatch platform. Stan saw Joey and waved. Joey waved back, but the governor had pushed his son along before he could see.

"Hey, move it along, brat," someone said behind Joey.

Joey didn't bother looking back as he stepped up to the next available hose. There was no point. He knew who it was. Michael was a surly, joyless man. Joey couldn't understand how his dad had been friends with this miserable wretch.

Joey grabbed the hose, pressing the red anodized nozzle into the front panel of his life support system. There was a metallic snap as the hose seated. And with a clean connection detected, the pump kicked on. Warm humidified air rushed into his suit. The tempest flipped his hair and fogged the inside of the glass helmet. After a few seconds, the fog faded.

The display built into the left forearm of the AGLS showed: Power 100%. HTP (high-test peroxide) 100%. Oxygen 100%. Water 100%.

Joey stepped away from the station, intentionally not acknowledging Michael. The man was a conversational quagmire.

"Joseph Junior," Foreman Kalil shouted.

"Yes, Foreman?"

"Section 85-90, Ring G today. Good luck, Joey."

"Got it. Have a good day," Joey said, and he walked down the ramp into the crater. The dig was divided into sections by radial lines. And each pie slice was further divided into concentric rings. The numbers 85-90 were the degrees off north, and G was the seventh ring in from the rim of the crater.

"Michael," Foreman Kalil shouted, "Section 85-90,

Ring H."

Joey groaned. Michael would be next to him, and the man never seemed to shut up. It wasn't any of the chanting work cadences people used to pass the day. It was just chatter, and most of that was complaining about other miners. Everyone complained and busted each other's chops, but there was joy and camaraderie in it. Michael's complaining was never good-natured.

But for now he was quiet. Before the silence would let his mind wander, Joey reminded himself to focus. He set down his shovel and brush and gripped his pickaxe.

"Hey, Junior," Michael said.

"Hi," said Joey, matching Michael's unfriendly tone. He heaved his pickaxe, swung it in a high overhead arc, and spiked the uneven ground. Rock spit from the impact, and Joey felt the satisfying shock through his hands.

"I heard you finally started digging in grids like a man," Michael said, not taking the hint. "You know, instead of a stowaway rat in the dry goods."

"Maybe you want to stand here running your mouth, but I'm getting to work."

Michael gave Joey a humorless smirk.

"Maybe you'll make it as a miner after all...But I doubt it."

Michael kept talking as Joey kept working. Joey tuned him out, and eventually, the miserable bastard stopped.

# CHAPTER NINE

Joey was three hundred seventy-seven hits into the day and lost in the thunking rhythm of the axe striking soil. This was being a good citizen. This was him being like his dad. But he didn't dwell on it, he just kept working.

On the four hundred and thirteenth swing, the pointed end of the pickaxe deflected against something hard and wedged into a crack. The jolt shot through his hands, elbows, and shoulders. He had to shake the feeling back into his fingers.

Veins of solid iron hurt like that, but this was different. *Different how?*

*Nothing unusual,* he cajoled himself.

The point of the pickaxe was wedged tight. He tugged hard on the handle with both hands. The axe broke free, pulling a near-perfect square of brittle rust-colored rock with it. *It's nothing,* he told himself, *just keep picking.*

He axed the square, a tentative hit. He didn't want to destroy it for some reason. After more cajoling, he hit it again. A layer of rock chipped away, revealing the corner of a dark glassy surface. A kind of transparent obsidian, backed by dark concrete. Joey stared. Under the surface were etched lines, and a dot glowing a rich cobalt blue. He put his hand close and the glow brightened, almost imperceptibly. But it was enough to light up the beige grip pads of his gloves. There was something else. Had he heard something? He hovered his hand over the dot again. The AGLS speakers faintly crackled and popped. He pulled his hand away and the speaker went silent again.

As his gaze was lost in the depth of the blue dot, the memory of the rogue asteroid of his youth called to him. The blue light he was told was not a light.

A battle erupted in Joey's mind. One faction screaming for him to get to work. The other screaming for him to investigate. He knew which faction he wanted to listen to, and that one must not win.

Joey looked around while working a patch of ground to the side of the mysterious square. The foremen were focused outward, as usual. Michael was dutifully chipping away at his patch of the crater. No one paid him any attention, and the temptation was too great. He pulled out his notebook and sketched a picture of the glassy corner.

To keep up the appearance of working, he shoveled rocks for a few minutes. But the battle in his mind was soon lost. That square of rock, and its corner with the glowing blue dot, would not let him be. He hit the square again. The top layer of rock flaked away completely, and Joey was transfixed.

The glowing blue dot was only one of dozens set in the glass, connected by a network of lines and circles.

Despite being buried under the asteroid surface for unknown ages, and being hit with a sharp pickaxe, the glass was free of any deep gouges or chips. There were only fine scratches that caught the light in swirling rings, and those seemed intentional.

Joey caught himself staring. Was it a decorative tile or something more? Not wanting to disappoint his dad two days in a row, he scratched at the ground with his pickaxe for a few minutes. He took surreptitious glances at the other miners, but they were busy with their patches of crater.

When it felt safe, he turned the page in his notebook and drew the whole tile in detail. With his grease pencil, he measured the etched lines and the distance between the dots. Two of the dots were bigger than the others. The lines, which had seemed random at first, connected the two bigger dots after passing through a handful of the smaller ones. There were circles etched around some, and they passed through still smaller dots.

Whatever this thing was, it was beautiful. He went back to his drawing and corrected a few things. He wrote notes and questions. Time to get back to—

"Hey, Junior!" Michael said. "What are you doing just standing around?"

Joey's stomach soured, his palms sweated. His dad would hear about this and be furious. He flipped his notebook closed and clipped it to the holder.

"Whoa. What is that?" Michael said, pointing his axe handle at the tile. "What are you doing, Squirt? You have to report anything like this right away."

Joey's mind churned. There were rules for the tiles?

That must mean there were more of them. Were they all like this one? Or were there other things? Bigger things?

"Foreman!" Michael shouted.

A foreman who was standing on the lip of the crater about fifty paces away turned. He motioned for another foreman to keep his watch and jogged over.

Joey's stomach knotted as he saw it was Foreman Ganyon. He didn't like Ganyon, and Ganyon didn't like anyone.

"Hey guys, what's the issue—" He cut off when he saw the tile. His eyes blazed. "Holy shit."

Ganyon pushed a button on the front of his suit. He spoke, but his voice didn't come through on Short-Coms.

Other miners noticed them standing there, and a handful broke protocol and walked over. Joey felt like he was falling.

"Keep your distance," Ganyon called out to the gathering miners. They stopped some twenty paces away.

"I called you over," Michael said. "Right away, I did. Right when I saw the boy looking at it."

Joey frowned at Michael.

"Oh?" Ganyon said.

"Yeah. He was writing in his notebook."

"Oh?" the foreman said again. His playful tone was a lie.

"We got ourselves an Olly," he said, loud enough for the other miners to hear.

They laughed, and Joey felt choking panic.

"Were you taking notes?" Ganyon's tone made

Joey feel small.

Joey looked around at all the eyes on him. By that time, thirty men and boys had gathered around him; more watched from a distance. One miner was not caught up in the distraction. Joey knew that would be his dad, still swinging away with his new pickaxe. Feeling embarrassed, he dropped his gaze to his feet.

"I was trying to help."

"Help?" Ganyon scoffed.

"Yeah," Joey said. "I wanted—"

"Can I get these notes? They may be helpful for our research team." The condescension was enraging.

Joey stared the foreman in the eye, defiance welling inside him. He did not want to give up his drawing. He was sure he was already going to be forced to give up the curious tile. Joey couldn't hold the stare. The foreman held his rifle in the low ready position now. Not slung barrel down as they normally did when talking to miners. Joey was so wrapped up in the injustice he hadn't noticed Ganyon shift the weapon.

"Now." All playfulness was gone.

Joey unclipped the notebook, thumbed through the pages until he saw the first drawing of the tile. He started to turn to the next page but stopped, grabbed the page of the first drawing, and pulled. The staccato vibration of the tough paper ripping from the spiral binding was like tearing off a finger. It was *his* drawing of *his* tile. Joey handed the paper to Ganyon.

Ganyon looked at the drawing. The foreman sneered.

"Ah," Ganyon said. "You're the one who draws. An Olly indeed."

The gathered miners laughed.

"Okay, everyone. Let's get back to it," Foreman Kalil said as he jogged over.

The miners turned away as instructed. The conversations as they walked back to their sections overlapped, but the point was clear. Joey was an Olly. And his dad would hear it. Of that he was sure.

The two foremen held buttons on their suits and talked privately. Kalil was calm while Ganyon fumed. They were pointing at Joey. In time, they broke away. Kalil gave Joey a tight smile and left.

"Michael," Ganyon said, "I'll mark you down for an extra dessert tonight."

Joey scowled at Michael. A dessert? That's what this was about?

"Thank you, Foreman," Michael said. He looked at Joey with a satisfied smile.

Ganyon turned back to Joey, regarding the boy like Joseph Senior had regarded his worn axe. But he controlled his anger, and the rifle was slung low again.

"Next time, don't trouble yourself, kid. We have experts for these things. Now go work Section 145-150, Ring H, so we can have someone clean this section."

"Yes, Foreman," Joey said. He looked at the tile. His treasure. Then he frowned and headed to the opposite end of the crater.

He passed a handful of foremen wheeling a cargo box toward the strange tile. There was a man with them who Joey had never seen. Like the governor, he looked different from the citizens of TMS. Behind wire-rimmed glasses, his dark eyes were deep set, with pillowy bags under them. He was the oldest person Joey had ever seen, and the most well-fed.

Joey got one last glimpse of the tile as the men loaded it into the cargo box. He wondered whether he'd ever see something like it again.

# CHAPTER TEN

In the river of miners heading for the equipment racks, Joey was swept along. It had been four hours since his discovery was taken away by foremen, and the well-fed old man. Four hours of feeling the injustice of it. The way he figured, the tile should be on the wall in his room, displayed with the same satisfaction of earning a Turnover, Spiced Apple.

He returned his equipment, and the river carried him past the Mushroom. The chatter of the crowd washed over him and he heard none of it.

"Attention, everyone," a voice cut into the chatter, overriding ShortComs.

All the miners stopped to listen.

"We are happy to announce that we are calling the dig today. Because of your hard work, we cleaned all the useful ore from the crater. Previous estimates had us finishing this crater in the next cycle. You'll have one extra free day before we prep for the hop to RN-1-2. And a bonus has been added to all your retirement funds."

The crowd of miners cheered.

"And I want to acknowledge Foremen Browning and Adams. This morning they intercepted another reffie raiding party. If you see them in the next few days, give them your thanks. In fact, give all the foremen your thanks for keeping us safe through another cycle."

The message ended with a little crackle and the crowd cheered again. Miners sought out nearby foremen, patting them on the back and thanking them for their service.

"Joey," Stan said.

Joey snapped out of his fog. He didn't even notice Stan walking up right in front of him. Stan wore a huge grin and was practically bouncing. Joey had never seen him look excited about anything.

"Hi," Joey said, "why are you smiling?"

Stan didn't answer. He scanned the crowd, then nudged Joey to move away. Past the anchoring cables of the Mushroom, and past the chatter coming over ShortComs, he finally spoke.

"You get all the fun, don't you?" Stan said.

Joey narrowed his eyes at Stan.

"The artifact!" Stan said.

"Arti—?" Joey said, then added, "Oh, the tile?"

"Friend, that was no tile." Stan was electric with excitement. "It's a marker. Like a road sign."

"What's that?" Joey said, still not caught up in Stan's enthusiasm. But Stan was unfazed.

"Think of it like a map. I broke into my father's study. He has a collection of books. It's not like a real library or anything that extravagant, it's only a couple hundred books. And! One of the books has pictures of a similar artifact—the tile. And other things like it. No one knows their true origin. Hell, they don't even know what they're made of. It might not even be human made. Each one of the little blue dots seems to be one of the asteroids in this cluster."

*Hundreds of books?* Joey had only ever seen one. The Book. *A library? A tile from people who were not human. A tile that's a map.*

"And. And..." Stan said, "it might be more than one thousand years old. Much more."

"A thousand years?" Joey couldn't even grasp the idea. "Can you imagine?"

"No, it's quite remarkable."

"Can I see the books?" Joey said.

"They're nothing," Stan said, suddenly reserved. "It's mostly just a bunch of boring repair manuals. A lot for equipment we don't even use anymore."

"So, then, if you don't need them anymore..."

Joey trailed off. He would not be allowed to see the books. He would not be allowed to *trouble himself.* A great weight settled on him. The weight of rules. The weight of having only one path open to him. The path with brittle gray rock and a pickaxe to swing at it. But he needed to adapt to that life for his dad, for himself, for the Society. He had to accept what his contribution was meant to be.

"Anyway. Who cares about the books, friend," Stan said with a sudden intensity. "I have something better. We're going to go."

"Go where?"

"To the tomb, silly," Stan said, then, "Oh, shit. I didn't tell you where the road sign takes you. Some signs like it pointed to ancient tombs. It's a place where rich rulers get put when they die. It's like a room with a person-shaped box inside. It's called a sarcophagus. So far, they've been empty. The book says they don't know, but I think they're aliens—people from another star. I didn't get a chance to look at all the pictures before my father came."

"I don't know what any of that means," Joey said. An alien tomb was as hard to fathom as a thousand years. Harder. But he had to pull himself back from the brink.

"I'll explain on the way," Stan said.

If Joey didn't get control of his thoughts, he'd be lost. He'd be an Olly through and through. *Don't be an Olly. Don't be an Olly.*

"I have to go," Joey said. "Dad will have supper on soon."

"Joey," Stan pleaded, "we have the four-day break, then we're packing for the jump to cluster RN-1-2 next week. It will be nearly three years before we come back to RN-3-4."

"I can't. I have to be a good citizen. I try really hard, but stuff keeps happening. And getting eaten by reffies won't help either."

Joey stalked away, head down, fighting back tears of frustration.

"Joey," Stan called out.

But Joey didn't look back. He was already in trouble with the foreman, and now he would have to face his dad.

# CHAPTER ELEVEN

Joey's eyes were glassy as he slid open the inner airlock door. Joseph Senior stood in the living room, arms folded. His dad was an Oscar, and Joey could never live up to that reputation. No matter what happened, something always pulled him away. When he met his dad's stern gaze, Joey's eyes filled with tears.

"Hey, hey. What's wrong, Joey?" Joseph Senior said. He walked over and wrapped his arms around Joey.

"I don't want you to be disappointed with me anymore," Joey said, sputtering while trying not to cry. "I don't want to be Olly."

Joseph Senior released Joey from the hug. He was confused.

"I'm not disappointed, son. In fact, I'm curious about something. So if anyone is Olly right now, it's me."

It was Joey's turn to be confused. He wiped the tears off his cheeks with the back of his hand.

"What?"

"How'd you know they was going to call the dig today?" Joseph Senior said.

This wasn't what Joey expected.

"I didn't," Joey sobbed. It sounded like he was going to be in trouble again.

"Yes, you did. You made like you was joking. But you weren't."

"How would I know—"

"Please, don't lie to me, son," Joseph Senior said.

"The rocks tell me," Joey said.

"What?" Joseph Senior was incredulous. "Are you hearing things?"

"They don't actually talk. I ain't a nut job. It's the colors, Dad. The sparkles in the sunlight. The way the axe goes in. All of that tells me. And when they process the ore, the machine says the thing I saw from the colors and other stuff. So when the colors change, it means the ore changes."

Regardless of what his dad said, Joey might as well have taken his grease pencil and written "OLLY" in big letters on his forehead. But his dad didn't get mad, and Joey's sobbing subsided.

"That's amazing," Joseph Senior said.

Joey was really confused now. Had his dad really seen value in the heresy against chapter three of The Book?

"It's pretty easy once you see it. I can show you."

Joseph Senior was lost in thought. Maybe he was impressed, or maybe he was conflicted about what to do with someone so far from Oscar. But Joey sensed an opening and took it.

"But, Dad," Joey said at last, "there's something even better. Something I found at the dig today. Better than ore."

Joseph Senior's head snapped up.

"That was you? And you called the foreman right away? Good for you, son."

Joey wasn't about to correct that record. Not while his dad was with him.

"It was a big square tile. As big as my chest. It was like glass, but dark, and there was these glowing blue dots inside it."

His dad frowned, his brow knitting in confusion.

"A tile? What kind of tile?"

"Stan said it's a map. He seen one in his dad's books. He's got hundreds of books, Dad, but they're all different. It's a map to a tomb, he says. I guess that's where fancy people get put when they're dead. They might not even be *people* people, like us. They might be people from another star. Like an alien or something. Stan wants to—"

Joey caught himself. *I may be Olly, but at least I'm not Michael.* A new idea struck him.

"Dad! We can go. We can go see the tomb. We have four days to go there and back."

"What?"

Whatever door of curiosity was opening in Joseph Senior slammed shut.

"We are not going anywhere."

"Is it against the rules?"

"I don't know. No one has been stupid enough to leave the colony to find out. Reffies, rogue rocks. Going to another asteroid. It's madness. You'll get eaten, or smashed, or drift out into space."

"It'll be three years before we come back."

"It doesn't matter. We are not going. Now, or in

three years. They'd start using our faces for Olly in your comic books! Assuming we survived. Which we wouldn't."

"But, Dad—"

"Why are we even discussing this? The answer is no. We're not gonna disrespect the Society that has given us all this." Joseph gestured to the apartment.

"Our three days are ours," Joey said, getting angry. "Chapter one. In the stupid Book."

"Joseph Junior! This conversation is over. This apartment, you having your own room, it's all because we are good miners, good citizens! We start chasing stars and they shove us in the small condos, or worse, the bunkhouses, and eating in the mess hall instead of our kitchen. No more fun dinners. We'll eat what everyone eats."

Joey's face tightened, and his shoulders sagged.

"You're gonna spend the next three days in your room," his dad continued, "and if I see you doing anything other than reading The Book, I will tear down all your drawings, and you won't be making any more."

Joey felt the constricting feeling of his suit running low on air. Not low on oxygen. Like some insidious joke, the lack of oxygen was a blissful, ignorant descent. When the air runs out, it's far worse. There isn't anything to draw into your lungs, and they feel like they're being sucked out of your chest. You get desperate to get out of the suit, which you absolutely must not do. It was a feeling he'd only experienced in training, but it left a deep scar of a memory.

# CHAPTER TWELVE

Joey lay in his bed with the stupid Book resting on his chest. It was all he could do to not tear out the pages. There would be no hiding that mess, and besides, his dad didn't let him close the door to his room.

He spent the last several hours looking not at the thin vellum pages but over the top of them and out the window. He drifted to sleep several times. Each time his eyes closed, the claustrophobic feeling returned and he snapped awake, gasping for air. He then stared out the window, and the cycle played out again.

This time when he awoke, his dad was snoring in the next room. Joey set The Book aside and grabbed his spiral-bound notebook. With his finger, he traced the lines on his drawing of the tile. Stan had said it was a map of the asteroid cluster. Joey had only caught glimpses of a foreman's map but recognized the crater and the TMS structures arranged around it.

He studied his drawing, trying to decipher the jumble of lines and circles and dots. It must mean something that two of the dots were bigger. Joey had been sure to capture that detail. Maybe one of them was the tomb, and the other was where they were now. Yes! If the tile was indeed what Stan had claimed, it made sense. One dot for where you were, the other for where you wanted to go. But which was which?

He got up and went to the window. RN-3b was crossing the sky at that moment. The slow rotation of RN-3a had his window aligned with several asteroids in the cluster. Some were so distant it was hard to tell them from dim stars. He looked at his drawing to compare. There was a pattern, a cluster of two asteroids, a solitary asteroid, then a cluster of three, and he found that pattern on the drawing. He imagined he was floating in space far above the cluster. That was it! The big dot near the lower corner of the tile, the one with the circle around it, it was RN-3a, and the dot on the circle must be RN-3b. The circles were orbits!

Joey wanted to shout. Could he get in contact with Stan somehow? Probably not. The grounds would be patrolled by foremen looking out for reffies. But it didn't matter. He had to try. There was no way he could go back to sleep, or back to mining again, until this itch was scratched.

He turned back to his bed, grabbed his notebook and pencil. The comic sat on the corner of his mattress. The illustration of Olly stared up from the cover, grinning stupidly as the rock runner was about to crush him.

Joey smiled.

With both hands, he eased the door to his room closed. He winced as the soft click of the latch tolled like a dropped pot in his ears. He whipped his head to look at Joseph Senior. He still snored. Joey let his breath go and pulled his dad's door closed.

In the kitchen, Joey opened the fridge. He grabbed one of the unmade meal kits. The package read Stew, Beef and Veggies. He tore open the tough plastic bag and ate the congealed stew cold. He didn't know when he'd get a full meal again. But they only ate once a day, so missing a couple meals seemed manageable. Next, he grabbed three snack blocks from the cupboard. He choked one of the gelatin cubes down right away. His eyes squeezed from the tartness. They weren't meant to be eaten like that, only nibbled.

He wrote something in his notebook, tore the page out, and left it next to the fridge.

He realized the buzzer would go off as soon as he opened the inner airlock door. He thought for a moment, then bit off half of one remaining snack block. Powering through the sour-fruit flavor, he chewed until it was soft and sticky, then smashed it against the buzzer. He swallowed the other half. The block did its job and left his mouth watering.

Joey took a deep breath and slid the door open. The buzzer sounded but it was muffled and faint. *I guess I'm really doing this*, he thought.

# Chapter Thirteen

Inside the chamber, Joey made sure the inner door was closed. He didn't know if the chewed snack block would stay stuck to the buzzer long, but it was easier to verify the exposed latch was secure from inside. He unhooked his Angel from the wall and the sanitation systems. He pressed the snack block onto the ridged pin next to the waterspout of the "snack bar" under the helmet seals.

The procedures for donning the suit were as familiar as walking. But Joey followed the steps printed on the airlock wall with elaborate care. He checked each clasp and seal, then checked them again, and again. *Olly did not check his equipment and it cost him dearly. I am not an Olly,* Joey thought. Olly never went off asteroid, but if he had, he wouldn't have checked his equipment like Joey did.

Even with his justification secure, if there was something more stupid Joey could be doing right now, he couldn't imagine it. This would be the first time he'd been out of his apartment without his dad knowing. He felt fear. Not the fear of the rogue asteroid passing overhead, or of the violence of the Trojans. This fear he chose. This fear was exciting.

He hit the large red button. The air pumped out of the chamber and his world went silent. His breathing and the quiet hum of the Angel's life support were the only sounds. When he moved, the suit creaked, the metal fittings slid against each other. Unless he ran into Stan, those sounds were going to be his only companions for the next few days.

He had to shove the outer airlock door open, its hinges still gritty with regolith. Of course they were. Because he hadn't cleaned them. He would have cleaned them as part of his morning chores. But in the morning, he would be gone.

He leaned his head out the doorway and looked up and down the row of apartments. He expected to see foremen patrolling or standing guard. But there were none.

He stepped over the threshold and planted his first unauthorized step outside.

What would a foreman do if they saw him? What would Joey say? Strict rules about being out at night were never discussed. Everyone stayed in as far as he knew, and they did so without needing to be told. Fear of reffies ensured that. Besides, the work was tiring, and neither Joey nor his dad ever stayed up late. Rules or not, something told him to not treat this excursion like his morning walk to work. He wouldn't be counting to pass the time. He was too keyed up.

Hung from the overhead cargo straps were blue-white globe lights. They were dimmer than normal, and their glow barely penetrated the black of the night. But still, if a patrolling foreman looked down the path, Joey would be spotted. Outside his bedroom window the ground was always dark, so he slipped through the narrow gap between apartments to get to the other side. He could hardly see his own boots now, and he dared not turn on the AGLS's work lights. The Mushroom was there in the distance, and just beyond was the first stop on this foolish trek.

He waved his hands in front of him; each step he took was cautious and probing. The cargo straps came off the apartments at forty-five degrees and were anchored to thick hooks set in concrete blocks. In the dim light, it would be very easy to trip over them. His tense breathing and thumping heart were all he could hear.

At the end of the row of apartments Joey leaned around the corner, again expecting patrolling foremen and seeing none. Joey followed the main path to the crater, staying just outside the glow of the low marker lights. As he got closer to the Mushroom he walked farther into the darkness. There was no way to tell if there was someone in the control room looking down on him. Without patrols, that would be the only way they could spot reffies.

Joey saw a surprisingly short foreman under the dome of the Mushroom. At first Joey was relieved. At least someone watched for reffies. But the foreman paced in circles like a bored child. Joey smiled. The foreman wouldn't be paying attention to the dig site.

Still avoiding the light, Joey worked his way to the recharge station. Each time the foreman's lazy circle put his back to Joey, the boy jogged.

The recharge station was dark. And the hum that vibrated the soles of Joey's boots wasn't there. Now what? All he ever did was plug the charge hose into his suit. The hoses had no other interface. Once connected, they did what they did automatically. When it was on.

There must be some sort of control panel. Unless it was operated from the Mushroom. If it was, his trip would be over.

He checked along the side of the hulking box. Under a set of gauges, he found a metal panel a little bigger than his gloved hand. It had no handles or visible latches. Things that had to be handled with pressurized gloves usually had simple operations. Joey shrugged and pushed in on the panel. He felt a soft click and the panel swung down. Inside were two large silicone-wrapped buttons. One red, one green. He took a deep breath.

"I knew you wouldn't be able to pass this up."

Stan stepped from behind the recharge station. This time it was his friend, but if Joey didn't keep his eyes open, he'd end up in a reffie's stew.

"Well, I was going to…" Joey shrugged.

"And now you're going to go without me? I've been pacing around the Mushroom for an hour."

"I thought you was a foreman."

Stan nodded.

"Fair enough. But what's your plan? How were you going to go?"

"You sound like a foreman."

"Sorry. I don't mean to. I'm actually curious."

"I figured out the map," Joey said. "What all the

dots and circles and lines mean. See. Before they stole the tile, I drew a picture of it. Every little part."

Joey opened his notebook. Stan smiled at the drawings as Joey flipped through the pages.

"The dots are the asteroids, right? These two bigger ones, here and here. The lower one is us, RN-3a. The other one is that tomb thing."

"Impressive."

"You mean that?"

"I do. But there are some things you didn't account for," Stan said, pointing at a wrist-thick insulated line that ran from the pumps. "See this cable? It's a monitoring line. If you'd turned this beast on, it would have lit up the control room in the tower."

"I was worried about that."

Stan smiled with pride.

"No need to worry. I disabled that system before I left. And fortunately for both of us, I spent the last several hours calculating the current positions of the asteroids. Even in the achingly slow time of the cosmos, the asteroids should have moved a lot in a thousand years, but somehow they didn't. Do you know what that means?"

Joey shook his head. There was almost nothing Stan had said that made sense to him.

"Me neither," Stan said with a shrug. "Either the asteroids haven't changed their relative positions in a thousand years, or the dots on the artifact are moving with them."

"Which is it?"

"Both of them are absurd. So pick whatever absurdity you like best. Did you know that the rogue asteroid actually changed the speed at which this rock spins?"

Joey shook his head.

"And it should have slowed our speed around the sun. Not a lot, but enough to cause RN-3a to fall out of orbit in a million years."

"That sounds like Joey Junior, Junior, Junior, Junior's problem."

"It's weird, is what it is. Because it didn't happen despite what the computers said should happen."

*Is it worth telling him I don't understand again?* Joey wondered.

"But," Stan said, "not to worry about that either way. I've programmed the whole trip into my arm computer."

Joey frowned at his drawing. He'd been very proud about figuring out the map, but he had something else exciting planned. An idea inspired by the comic book. *I guess my dad should have got me something based on chapter four.*

"Okay. The big question. Who's driving the rock runner? Or are we taking the cycles?"

"Sorry, none of those will work."

"What? Why?"

"First, they're not easy to operate. It takes a year of training to become a pilot."

Joey sagged.

"But that's not the main reason."

"Oh?"

"They have tracking beacons. As soon as they know one is missing, they zero in on its position."

"All you keep telling me is how nothing is gonna

work. Since you don't like my plan. What do we do?"

"It'll be easier to show you. And for the record, I like your plan. The rock runner would get us there in half a day. But there's a bright side."

Joey wasn't satisfied.

"Trust me. It will be a grand adventure."

"I don't know what that is."

"In books, people are always going on big trips to foreign lands. Fighting monsters and stuff."

"I've only read The Book."

"Oh," Stan said. He was quiet for a long moment. Then he shrugged and said, "Let's go."

With a grandiose flourish, Stan reached into the control box and pressed the green button. It lit up, and the low hum traveled through the soles of Joey's boots. Small indicator lights illuminated each hanging hose as they came online.

The dangerous excitement surged as Joey snapped the charging hose into the front of his suit. The familiar click and rush of humidified air fogged his helmet. And as the fog faded, it was as if he walked through a door opened to the whole universe.

The fog in Stan's helmet faded. Their eyes met, and the two boys knew they were committed to this.

I *am not* Olly, Joey thought. But he was not convinced.

## Chapter Fourteen

In the darkness beyond the lights of the colony, the boys walked through the crater and out the other side. They passed the ruined foreman outpost, and Joey understood the horror of the Trojans in the crater was only a fraction of it. Shattered machinery littered a field that looked scraped by a million pickaxes.

"Did the foremen out here die?" Joey asked.

"No, they were evacuated," Stan said.

"Why didn't they evacuate the crater?"

"The computers were wrong about the size of the Trojan cloud. They thought the outpost might get light damage, at worst."

The boys fell into silence as they weaved their way around the debris. The Angel's work lights only lit the ground about thirty paces in front of them. Beyond that was black. Joey had the urge to draw the carnage, and the light from the unseen sun streaking through the clouds of ejecta. Stars twinkled through the dust from a million lifetimes away. So much destruction and so much beauty to capture in grease pencil, but they had a lot of walking to do.

He picked up the occasional rock, inspected it for interesting colors, then threw it along the ground. The rocks skipped along and vanished into the blackness. In the low gravity, some launched off the uneven surface high above the ground. Joey chuckled. Stan watched him with curiosity.

Joey found one fist-sized rock with the blue sparkles. He turned it over in his hand, watching the work lights play over its surface. Some ore they missed.

"You remind me of our geologists," Stan said. "They'd look at boring gray rocks like Oscar himself was hidden in them."

"Who did?"

"Geologists," Stan said. "They're the people who study the rocks. They direct where we dig."

"Oh," said Joey. He held the rock up to Stan. "Do they know about the blue sparkles?"

"I would imagine they do. I'm sure they even told me about it once. But my mind is usually somewhere else."

"When we get back, can you ask them about it? See, I saw when there's a lot of blue sparkles, the number on the ore machines is bigger. We dig a lot of rocks that don't have any ore at all. And then we leave all these chunks out here."

Stan stared at Joey like he was the alien artifact. After a moment, he snapped out of it.

"Who says I'm going back," Stan said.

"What?"

Stan snatched the rock from Joey's hand.

"Do you think I can throw it off the asteroid?"

"No," Joey said.

"Just like that. Just no?"

"Yeah. Just no. Me and Dad was just talking about that at supper the other day. He said on big asteroids the rock always comes back down. But it can take hours."

"You and your dad eat together all the time?"

"Every night," said Joey.

Stan threw the rock. It flew high before arcing back to the ground.

"You call that a throw?" Joey laughed.

"I barely tried. I'll show you."

"No. It's my turn. I'll show you."

Joey ran for the rock, and Stan chased him.

"No way. I bet I get to it first."

They chased each other around, dodging and grabbing for the rock. Joey managed to get it first and threw it.

"That was way higher."

"Not a chance. Anyway, I barely tried. So my next one is going all the way to Mars."

They laughed and chased after the rock again. Running toward the edge of the void.

## CHAPTER FIFTEEN

Joseph Senior woke at two in the morning. His sleep had been restless, and now it was gone.

When he was his son's age, Joseph fought the same restless feelings. In time, he learned to quiet them with The Book. He could not draw like his son, but his own father had taught him to see all the stories in The Book like they were his own memories. In them, he witnessed the mistakes of Olly as if he were Oscar. Joseph tried to teach his son the same way, but Joey had fun imagining all the different ways the stories could play out. They would laugh at the possibilities, but Joseph always tried to steer reading back to the meaning of The Book.

Sometimes, Joseph missed the low responsibility of youth. Michael, Felix, and he used to go out to the fields and try to throw rocks off the asteroid. They'd run around until the low oxygen alarms in their suits sounded. This was before the AGLS Mark I, and the reserves were much smaller. The artificial gravity wasn't as sophisticated, and they could float ten meters with each step. It was fun, but brittle bones were the price for that fun. It was only with the AGLS that retirement to Earth was possible.

On one of those outings, Felix had been so lost in the euphoria of oxygen deprivation that Michael and Joseph had to carry him. Felix was never as fun after that. He became brooding and quiet. They turned twelve and started mining, so it all got pushed aside. Felix did his job, and he did it with excellence and without complaint. But he was a machine going about its task. There was an emptiness in his eyes. If Joseph asked him about it, Felix would change the subject.

When they turned eighteen and they were finally allowed in the commissary bar, Felix drank too much too many times, and got into too many fights. They were hardly the first drunken fights at the bar, but they were the last. Soon after, the bar began serving alcohol-free drinks.

The door alarm snapped Joseph out of his reverie. He jumped up and yanked the room door open. Curious. He was sure he had left it open last night. Joey's door was closed too. He'd deal with that after the door alarm.

Two foremen were in the airlock chamber. Foreman Hagen, who Joseph knew, waved to Joseph through the window. The other foreman he did not know. Joseph jogged over and slid the door open, noting that the inner lock was not engaged.

As the foremen walked in, Joseph noticed a chewed piece of snack block on the ground. Before he had time to think about the growing list of mysteries, the foremen were inside his kitchen.

"Sorry to wake you, Joseph," Foreman Hagen's

voice came through the exterior speaker on the front of the AGLS. There was a crackle as the speaker cut off.

"Foreman Hagen!" Joesph said. "Ain't seen you in ages. Thought you retired."

"Hell, I wish," Hagen said. "I'm night shift now. It's much quieter. I sit in the Mushroom. I read and wait for some red light to flash to tell me something's up."

"Sounds a little boring."

"Yeah, just the way I like it."

Joseph chuckled.

"Oh, sorry. Manners. This is Foreman Rickman." Hagen motioned to the other foreman. "He's the new kid, so feel free to give him a hard time."

"I'm not new." Rickman chuckled. "I just trans-ferred from transport."

"That's even worse, new kid," Hagen said with a laugh.

"Good to meet you," Joseph said. He wanted to end the suspense. "Anyway, what can I do for you?"

"Oh, Stan, the governor's son, wasn't in his room, or anywhere else in the Mushroom. Probably out dicking around in the fields or something. But since we see him talking to Joey a lot, we thought maybe he'd know where the kid got to."

"Right. I'll go wake him." Joseph said.

Joseph opened Joey's room. Thoughts of last night's conversation came crashing in when he saw the empty bed. *What are you up to, son?* He turned to Hagen with a shrug.

"He's not here."

The two foremen looked at each other.

"Can you get suited and come with us?" Hagen

said apologetically.

"Of course. Is it okay if I get a snack first? I skipped dinner." *Because my son was talking about looking for aliens.*

"No problem. Like I said, the kids are probably throwing rocks in the field like we all used to."

There was no worry in Hagen's voice.

"You want anything?" Joseph asked. His voice shook slightly.

"Thanks. I don't want to go through the hassle of taking this thing off." He rapped his knuckles on his glass dome.

Joseph opened the refrigerator and saw Joey's note on the counter.

It read, "Our three days are ours."

The gnawing worry turned into biting.

# CHAPTER SIXTEEN

After they had been walking uphill for some time, and when the dust clouds shone bright with sunlight, Joey and Stan came to a sharp drop-off, a cliff with no bottom. Below the edge of the irregular-shaped asteroid was space. Logic told him if he fell, he would roll along the ground, but his imagination saw a step off that edge as a step into the void. It was the same void that was always around him, but he felt the emptiness of it in the pit of his stomach.

"Now what?" Joey said.

"Now we jump."

"Jump?"

"Yep. Give me the rock." Stan held out his hand.

Joey handed the rock over and Stan hurled it straight out. It flew farther away from the surface than any of their earlier throws. It slowed and seemed to hang in place for a long moment before falling back toward the underside of the precipice. The way the rock flew was bending his mind. Between that and the drop-off, Joey felt nauseous.

"Freaky, isn't it?" Stan said, standing close to the

edge and seeming unconcerned. He checked his forearm computer. Then with his foot he drew an arrow in the dust pointing off the cliff. He checked the computer again, wiped the arrow away, then redrew it. He looked at Joey with a satisfied smile. But Joey didn't get what the older boy was up to.

"In twelves minutes we have to jump right along this line. That should put us right in the path of RN-3b, the largest satellite moon to the rock we are on now."

Joey stared at him. The danger part of the dangerous excitement was taking over.

"Don't worry. I spent the whole evening calculating this. It will be like cake."

"This is stupid," Joey said.

"What did you think this trip would be? Your plan was to endeavor to another asteroid, right? At some point, that logically means you must, you know, go to another asteroid."

"You're going to make a good foreman," Joey said sourly. "I wanted to take a rock runner. See something new before we move to RN-1-2."

"I promise you," Stan said dryly, "RN-1-2 is exactly as boring as this rock. But as to seeing something new, friend, that's going to require you to jump. And now we have eight minutes."

"How? You still haven't said how."

"We use the Angel's jump system."

Joey stared at him.

"The micro thrusters," he continued. "If you stomp the left heel of your boot hard into the ground, you'll have ten seconds to jump, and it will help you jump really, really high."

"Really?"

"Really. The thrusters reset eventually and bring you back down. Unless! You get closer to another source of gravity."

"Like another asteroid?" Joey exclaimed.

"Like another asteroid."

"Why don't I know about this?"

"I guess they don't tell you unless it's relevant to your job," Stan said with a shrug.

"Then why do you know?"

"I guess they think I'll need to know what everyone's job is since"—Stan put on a comical manly voice—"one day, son, you too shall run for governor, and rest assured, you will win."

Joey laughed. He wanted to ask another question. He wanted to push the jump off longer.

"Now. You need to try a small jump so you see what it's like. Come away from the edge, stomp your left heel, and jump straight up. Not too hard. In fact, just stand up quickly. But do it now."

Joey took a nervous breath and stomped his foot. A short metallic beep sounded in his suit. He squatted down and thrust up. He launched himself well over Stan's head, laughing with the thrill of it. And when he came down, the landing jolted him.

"Landing hurt a little."

"Don't worry. The system is there to simulate Earth's gravity. It won't let you get hurt, assuming you land right. Now, we have to go. Don't forget to stomp your boot again. It resets every time."

"You go first. Show me."

"The jump window is too narrow. We have to go

now. Stomp!"

Stan grabbed hold of Joey's arm. He stomped his foot. Joey copied him, and before he could think, Stan ran, pulling Joey with him.

"JUMP!"

They jumped off the precipice and out into the void. Stan still held Joey's arm. Joey looked back to see the safety of RN-3a shrinking away fast. Joey's mind exploded with excitement and terror. The micro thrusters usually fired short, unnoticed bursts. Now, the gritty hum of HTP passing over the tiny silver catalyst mesh in the micro thrusters was constant. Their tiny vibrations tickled.

"There!" Stan shouted. He pointed to RN-3b drifting in front of them.

The thrusters slowed, and the hum ceased. The boys seem to hang at the midpoint between the two asteroids for a long time.

"Stan! What do we do?"

Stan didn't answer. He wore the biggest smile Joey had ever seen on a person. Then a flurry of little bursts from the micro thrusters came, and they were whipped upside down. Or right side up for RN-3b. And slowly they built speed, heading feetfirst toward the smaller asteroid. Joey laughed and Stan whooped with delight.

"Ha ha! Yes!" Stan shouted. "Get ready to land. Remember to protect your dome!"

He gave Joey a gentle shove. They were now several meters apart. And the surface of RN-3b rushed toward them. Joey felt the thrusters kick in hard to slow their descent. He screamed, then grunted as his legs absorbed the impact. He went all the way to his hands and knees, winded and laughing from the sensory assault.

He tried to stand. It took a dizzy moment to get his balance. And longer still to get his bearings.

Stan sat on the ground nearby, looking quite pleased with himself. Their eyes met and they laughed at the insanity of what they just did.

"Stan," Joey said.

"Yes, friend."

"That was amazing!"

"Truly. And that was the easy jump. They only get more fun from here."

# CHAPTER SEVENTEEN

Joseph was led by Hagen and Rickman up the spiral stairs inside the Mushroom. He was out of his Angel and dressed only in his sleeping clothes. They had to strip out of their Angel, and go through a multistep dust-cleaning process that made the hassle of going into his apartment seem like nothing.

"You have to do this every time?" Joseph said, wiggling his fingers in his ears and working his jaw. The relentless blasts of air left his ears ringing and his eyes dry.

"Yeah. There's a lot of sensitive equipment inside," Hagen said. "Even after a hundred years of advances, regolith is murder."

"It wasn't like that last time I was here," Joseph said. His life was beautifully simple. He was thankful someone else took care of this part of the operation.

"When was that?" Rickman said.

"When I learned I was going to be a father."

"Right," Hagen said, "that was a different Mushroom then. Was that Aldus still?"

"Yeah," Joesph said. "Stanford was still a foreman."

The mood was collegial when Joseph and the foremen entered Governor Emerson's office. The governor was also in his sleeping clothes, but he did not look as worried as Joseph felt.

"Hello, Joseph," the governor said, then he turned to the foremen. "I asked for Joseph Junior."

"My boy is missing too," Joseph Senior said.

"Ah. It crossed my mind that they might be together. They're always talking, those two. But yesterday at the end of the shift, Foreman Salvadore said they seemed quite animated about something."

The governor rubbed his face.

"Do you know anything?" he asked Joseph.

"No."

Joseph wasn't used to keeping things from anyone, and the way the governor stared at him made him self-conscious. But Joey's plan to visit some tomb was so preposterous it didn't seem worth mentioning. The boys would be found any minute now.

The governor broke his stare and threw his hands up like the whole thing was only a minor inconvenience.

"Well, we shouldn't get too animated ourselves. We called the dig, so there's no production loss. Besides, they couldn't have gone too far. They'd both be on yesterday's charge."

"Governor," Hagen said, "I hadn't got a chance to tell you yet. We found the recharge station had been turned on. The tank levels are consistent with two suits being charged since last shift."

"What?" the governor growled. "Hagen, were you asleep in the control deck?"

"I was not, sir. No alarm went off. I invite you to check the system logs."

"No, no, I trust you, Hagen. Forgive my outburst."

"Not a problem, sir. But we should check the logs anyway. We may be able to see why the alarm didn't go off."

"Good point. So much for the late morning I promised the techs. Anyway. Joseph, thank you for your time. Don't worry. With a full suit, they won't get into too much trouble. Not like you and Felix when you were kids. This rock is big, but you could walk around the equator in a day or two, I suspect."

Felix was dead, killed only two days ago, and it was like it never happened. Joseph's old friend was reduced to an anecdote about kids getting into trouble.

"I think Hagen is right." Joseph sighed. "They probably just went to throw rocks into orbit. I think we all tried that a few times."

"I still try it sometimes," Hagen said. "We already sent out rock pilots. They should be able to fly the whole asteroid in a couple hours."

Joseph headed for the door. He stopped and look back at the governor.

"Please let me know as soon as you find him," Joseph said. "He's going to have some reading to do."

"Of course," the governor said.

## Chapter Eighteen

Joey was getting used to the terrifying thrill of the micro thrusters flipping him around, up abruptly becoming down. And he enjoyed the way his heart pounded as he leapt from one asteroid and during the mad fall to the next. But in the dead zone, where they neither flew away nor toward anything, he became desperate. With nothing to judge distance against, the stars seemed to close in until they were right in front of his face. He felt claustrophobic and disconnected from anything tangible at the same time. He longed for solid ground, and for the comfort of his dad sleeping in the room next to him.

Of the three jumps they'd made so far, this was the farthest. The micro thruster spurted puffs of vapor in every direction, keeping them in the void between asteroids RN-3f and RN-4a. Stan was twenty meters away, fixated on his forearm computer. The huge grin he wore all morning was gone. Joey looked at his own computer. The wireframe gravity indication arrow flipped around like an uncapped air hose.

"Why aren't we falling?" Joey said.

"The gravity sensor can't decide which asteroid it likes most. We may get pulled back to RN-3f."

"Are we stuck?"

Stan didn't answer.

"We should have jumped for the moonlet first," Joey said.

"Waiting on that orbit would have taken an extra two hours."

"That's better than this."

"We just need it to grab one or the other."

"How do we get it to do that?"

"We could vent the Angel. The escaping air would be like a thruster."

"And we'd be dead."

"Not if we could close the vent right after."

"How right after?"

"Instantly," Stan said, sounding hopeless. "I mean instantly. The button is very hard to push for a reason."

"If we could hit each other's heel..." Joey trailed off. They were only a few paces apart, but it was an unbridgeable gulf.

Desperate, Stan thrashed his body around, swinging his arms and legs toward RN-4b. His grunts broke through ShortComs. Stan checked his computer again.

"Yes! Do what I did. Throw your arms and legs toward RN-4a. Just hope Newton is on your side."

Joey watched Stan's almost imperceptible drift away. He copied Stan's spastic flailing. The gravity indicator steadied, only flipping occasionally. He threw his arms and legs around again, and the arrow pointed at RN-4a.

If he was falling, it was too slow to perceive. Stan

drifted away, or was Joey drifting back toward RN-3f? He focused on the arrow on his computer, reminding himself that he was indeed falling, and when he looked up, RN-4a was closer. And closer.

Desperation was replaced by the joyful terror of falling. And when Stan and Joey had rock under their feet again and the adrenaline faded, his legs trembled.

Despite the suit's compensation, it took a moment for his equilibrium to right itself. RN-4a was half the mass of the rock he had called home the last few months. But the Angel did its job and kept him on his feet.

"Now what?" Joey said, fighting the urge to lie down. He would have been asleep right now if it wasn't for the fool quest.

"Give me a minute." Stan held up his hand for silence and focused on his computer.

Joey shrugged. He opened his notebook to the drawing of the tile. He added a small checkmark next to the dots for each asteroid they'd landed on.

He looked back toward RN-3a, the place where they had started. The asteroid was so small in his vision now that he could block it with his outstretched fist. Sunlight spilled over the mining colony and glinted off the white structures. *They'll know we're gone soon.*

Joey turned back to the surface. The sun was directly behind him, sending his shadow stretching out to the short horizon. He waved his arms around and laughed. The shadow looked monstrous.

"Look how long my shadow is. It's like I'm a hundred meters tall."

Stan jumped to his feet.

"Crap! We should get off this plain!" he said. "Our shadows will be visible to patrols for kilometers."

Joey's stomach knotted. It hadn't occurred to him they might be running from TMS, from foremen. In that moment, he saw his dad's disappointed face. He saw the governor scowling at him. He heard Foreman Ganyon call him Olly, and the gathered crowd laughing. *What am I doing?*

Stan scanned the horizon. He checked his computer and pointed.

"There. That ridge over there, should be the lip of a crater."

Stan pushed Joey toward the crater and the boys moved. Joey found himself walking faster and faster.

"Not too fast," Stan said. "We need to conserve oxygen."

The boys fell silent as they kept a purposeful pace. In time, the idea they'd get caught faded. But the vision of Joseph Senior's disappointed face lingered. Halfway across the plain, and wanting a distraction, Joey picked up a rock.

"This one's going into orbit for sure," Joey said.

"No way. I've seen your throws," Stan said.

Joey threw the rock. But he didn't see where it went. His attention was drawn to a dark shape, gliding low on the horizon, occluding the stars beyond.

"Do you see that?" he said.

"Yeah," Stan said, inspecting his forearm computer. "It must be a rogue."

The dark shape slowed, and the sunlight caught the edge of its boxy bulk as it turned. It moved again, oozing forward above the ground and directly for them.

"It's a transport," Joey said.

"Yeah, not one of ours," Stan said. "Run!"

"Who else wou—"

Stan shoved Joey, and the boys ran.

Sweat poured into the moisture collectors, and each heaving breath fogged the glass in front of Joey's face. He looked over his shoulder. The transport was still coming.

"Get to the crater," Stan yelled and ran harder.

They scrambled up the slope as fast as they dared. Running, stumbling over broken rock toward the rim of the crater. The Angel's antifog system couldn't keep up with their hot breath. And their panting carried over ShortComs.

At the rim, they hurled themselves over the edge and ran along the shadowed inner wall until they found a hollow in a pile of boulders. They squeezed themselves under a shallow overhang and waited to be dragged out and cooked in a stew.

# CHAPTER NINETEEN

Their heavy breathing was the only sound as the ship passed overhead. The hull wasn't the pristine, sleek shape of TMS vehicles. It was rusty and battle scarred, a boxy utilitarian craft not built for aesthetics. If it had seen them, they couldn't tell. And they dared not look to see if it was turning.

"How is that thing still flying?" Stan whispered.

"You know who it is?"

"Not who, just the ship. I had a model of one. It's an old troop transport, from before the Hundred Year Peace."

"Hundred Year Peace?"

"Yeah. We're actually on year one seventy-three. There have been no major wars," Stan said.

Joey could only nod at the flood of new words and new concepts. Anyway, there was only one thing about the ship that worried him.

"You think it's reffies?" Joey said, still trying to catch his breath.

"Could be. I guess we'll find out when they serve our brains for dinner."

"They eat brains?"

"Duh, what else would they eat?"

"I figured they'd eat the muscles," Joey said. "You know, like a juicy arm or thigh."

The boys laughed, breaking their anxiousness.

"Nah, they'd eat the brains to make themselves smarter."

"Eating the brains of two dummies who jumped off an asteroid?"

"Good point," Stan said, then his voice took on an ominous tone. "If they're eating each other because that's their only food, then it means they'd have to eat everything."

"Everything?"

"Yeah, everything. Including all the gross parts."

Joey snorted with laughter.

"Well. I guess when they have Stew, comma, Joey's Butt, that will be my revenge."

Joey snorted again. Stan's laughing came out in a wheeze.

"You have a funny laugh," Stan said.

"You should talk." Joey barely got the words out in between snorts. "You sound like a ripped door seal."

The boys snorted and wheezed again. The sound of their own laughter fed on itself until their sides hurt and they were left panting.

"I can't wait to tell Dad about this," Joey said after a long moment. "He's gonna be mad. But after he makes me read the whole Book like fifty times, I'll tell him the whole thing while we eat dinner."

Stan was quiet. In the silence, Joey began to miss his dad a lot.

"Did I tell you how he mixes the meals up?" Joey said. Talking about him made his dad feel closer.

Stan shrugged.

"He takes stuff from all the different meals for the week and switches packets around."

"What do you mean?"

"Like we get spaghetti that has this tomato sauce. Only he uses the tomato sauce for the hamburger. And we have the spaghetti with butter and chicken instead."

"Curious," Stan said.

"It's the only thing I seen him do where he don't follow the instructions."

"Really?"

"Yeah. I asked him about it once. He said, I guess we're all a little Olly."

Stan laughed.

"What?" Joey said.

"He's right about that," Stan said. "This trip is putting us in the Olly Hall of Infamy."

"What does your dad make you?"

"My food is brought from the mess hall."

"Oh. I guess that gives you more time to sit together."

"No. We never eat together," Stan said. "Almost never."

"If we don't end up floating off to Mars, when we get back I bet both our dads give us big hugs."

"I don't want to go back," Stan said.

"That's why you know so much about the reffie diet. You wanna be one?"

"I might have to for a while. I've always wondered

what ears tasted like. Maybe your dad will know the right seasoning packet to use."

"Noodles would be good with ear."

Joey laughed again. Stan did not.

"I want to have an adventure."

"With monsters?"

"That sounds better than learning how to requisition O-rings," Stan said.

"Okay, where do we find monsters?"

Stan leaned forward, his voice low like someone might be listening.

"Once we get to the tomb—if that's even what it is—we might be far enough away for this to call the Earth-Mars transport before the Society can respond. See this."

Stan pointed to a box on his belt line. There was a metal flap held closed with a piece of aluminized repair tape.

"What is it?"

"It's an ELT. Emergency location transmitter. In case you need to be rescued."

Joey patted his own belt line where there was no ELT.

"The tape is to make sure we don't hit it too early. We have to time it right."

"For what?"

"To get back to TMS after we see the tomb. If we want to."

"If we want to?"

"There's another possibility. One for a real adventure. If we hit the ELT about an hour or two after we get to the tomb, there's a chance one of the cargo runners will pick up the signal. We'll be right in the path of the Earth-Mars regular."

"Whoa, I ain't that Olly. Once I see this tomb, I'm going back to my dad."

"Then while I'm waving to you from the Earth-Mars transport, you can wait for TMS to show up."

Joey laughed.

"Okay. What should I tell them about you?"

"Tell them I went on an epic adventure."

"Like in the books?"

"Exactly."

"Tell me about one of them."

"Which one? There are so many. My favorites are from before men could even leave Earth. Like *The Adventures of Tom Sawyer*. He's a poor kid who causes all kinds of trouble, but he's clever so he gets away with it. Then Tom Sawyer's friend Huck Finn goes on adventures too. He travels down a river with...Oh, and *Treasure Island*. There are gun fights with pirates, and kidnappers."

Joey was lost again. It often sounded like Stan was speaking another language, and in the couple minutes a day they usually got to talk, it was a novelty. Out here, where they had nothing but time, he wished he had more than a miner's knowledge. But if nothing else, the joy Stan had in telling about the books was infectious.

"I want to read about these guys."

"When we get to Mars we can find a library. There are thousands of books."

"Well, if TMS shows up first, you can lend me your *Adventures of Tom* book."

Stan looked away.

"What?"

"Nothing. I think maybe I'm getting tired."

Just the mention of being tired triggered a jaw-creaking yawn.

"Me too," Joey said, then looked at his forearm computer. Oxygen 57%. HTP 59%. Battery 80%.

"Running used a lot of juice," he said. "Are you sure we can make it all the way?"

Stan didn't bother looking at his computer.

"Yeah. I figured we would have to recharge. Throughout this cluster there are old oxygen wells and recharge stations. We have to detour to another rock. It should only add a couple hours to the trip."

"Will it still work?"

Stan shrugged.

"If reffies took the pumps, I brought a portable unit." Stan patted an extension box at the bottom of his life support unit. "Connecting straight to the well will be tricky. It would be easy to over-pressurize the suit."

Joey nodded; he would have to trust Stan. Even if he wanted to go back now, he would have just enough juice in his Angel to make it.

"Anyway"—Stan yawned—"let's tether up here and sleep. We can head for a charge in the morning."

"Okay," Joey said through a yawn.

The boys fastened anchor straps to the rocks and lay back.

Joey's mind popped from thoughts about his dad, to TMS, to the alien tomb, never landing on one long enough to sort anything out. He didn't think he'd ever get to sleep, but the long day caught up to him before he realized.

# CHAPTER TWENTY

J oseph Senior paced at the base of the Mushroom. Joey had been gone for a day now, and no one had told him anything. Each time he asked, he had to suit up and walk around until he found foremen. All they ever told him was that it was being handled. They were friendly and completely unhelpful. Except for Foreman Ganyon. Running into him had left Joseph seething.

"I'm not Olly's babysitter," Ganyon had said.

And now his AGLS was getting low on oxygen. Soon he'd be trying to walk around with only what air the shell could hold, and that would give him maybe twenty or thirty minutes. But that's what Joey could be facing right now. And damn it, Stan too. No one seemed concerned about any of it.

The hatch at the base of the Mushroom opened. The governor came out, flanked by Hagen and Ganyon, and they were followed by Michael.

"I want to help," Joseph Senior said.

"Help?" the governor scoffed. "I think you've helped quite enough with your mismanagement of the upbringing of young Joey. Our society needs him to be a miner, and a good one."

"What are you talking about? Joey's the top miner in the twelve-year-old group."

"When he's not kidnapping my son, perhaps."

"Joey didn't kidnap anyone."

"We have a witness."

"What? Who?"

Joseph looked at Michael, and Michael looked away.

"You asshole. What did you say?"

"Only the truth."

Joseph shoved Michael to the ground and was lunging for him when Hagen grabbed him. The governor jumped back to keep himself clear of the fight. Ganyon stepped in front of the governor with his rifle ready.

"Put the rifle down," Emerson said.

Ganyon lowered the rifle only a little. His grip was still tight, still ready.

"Joseph," Hagen said, "relax. This isn't going to fix anything."

"Stan put the idea into Joey's head," Joseph said. "He was talking about some sort of map."

Ganyon's eyebrows shot up. He looked back at the governor.

"Map?" Emerson said. "Map to what?"

"I don't know. Something he found at the dig. I told him to get his head straight and read from The Book."

"I told you Stan had been in the lab," Ganyon said.

"Tell me exactly what he told you," the governor said.

"I will, as soon as Michael tells me what was worth being a lying rat."

Michael raised himself to one knee and looked at Joseph, but he said nothing, his jaw set in defiance.

"Extra desserts for a month." The governor laughed. The low price of betrayal seem to amuse him.

Joseph seethed. He was going to have to do something, whether TMS allowed it or not. He couldn't stomach being idle while Joey was missing. Was that Olly or Oscar? He didn't care.

# CHAPTER TWENTY-ONE

Joey fought the urge to gulp water when he woke. It seemed all the strength he felt from swinging a pickaxe all day mattered little to running in panic. His skin was sticky with old sweat, and there was nothing he could do about it. At least the Angel's air scrubbers took care of the odor.

He sipped just enough water to wet his tongue, then bit a small piece off the snack block. The sticky, fruit-flavored gelatin made his mouth water, soothing his dry throat.

As he lay there waiting for Stan to wake, he tried to focus on the tomb, and jumps, and the fun ahead. But he was failing. He was supposed to be cleaning, preparing for the hop to RN-1-2, and reading The Book. All he could think about was what he wasn't doing, what he was meant to be doing.

He was relieved when Stan woke, and they climbed out of the crater to get the day going.

"Thankfully, the detour I mentioned looks like a quick couple of jumps."

"Okay," Joey said. Nothing Stan had done so far

had put them in danger. Nothing, assuming he forgot about jumping kilometers through empty space. But still he felt unease from being at Stan's mercy. In reality, he was always at someone's mercy—TMS's. Thankfully, they took good care of them. *And how are you showing them thanks?*

They jumped to another asteroid. And then another. In between, they walked and walked. And finally, Stan said they were near the oxygen well and, hopefully, a working recharge station. Good thing too. Joey's oxygen was down to 35%.

For an hour they slogged up a long slope, mangled by small overlapping craters. Some were ancient, pulverized by a million years of cosmic rays into vague circular ridges and barely high enough to trip over. Others were fresh and deep enough they had to be walked around. Some were from glancing impacts that left only shallow furrows. Others were created with rock-melting violence.

"How much longer until we get to the tomb?" Joey asked.

"Another ten or twelve hours, I'd guess."

*One full shift at the dig,* Joey thought.

"Jeez," he sighed, "that's forever."

"Who cares, friend," Stan said. His smile was big as ever as he spread his arms wide. "This is the good part."

"I thought you hated the *boring* gray rock."

"I'm not talking about the rock. I'm talking about the adventure. Two friends on an epic quest. The freedom of the open road."

"You're gonna have to start telling me what all the

words mean. Assume I don't know what any of them are. Because I don't."

"It means you and I are out here. On our own. Sleeping under the stars like in the books. And nobody's telling us to study pricing tables."

"Or to read about Olly," Joey said.

"Exactly!"

Joey's stomach growled.

"In your books, what do they eat?"

"They hunt rabbit and deer and stuff," Stan said excitedly. "Or they make a snare along a game trail, and they cook stuff on an open fire."

"Whatever all that is, it sounds more filling than a nibble from a snack block."

"But not as filling as ear with noodles." Stan laughed.

Then Stan pointed. He checked his arm computer again.

"See that crater ahead?" Stan said. "That's where the well should be. It's an older well, but my research says the connection is the same. If my research is wrong then...I guess we'll be hitting the ELT."

"Let's hope it works," Joey said. "I don't wanna get in trouble if I didn't even get to eat rabbit or see the tomb."

Stan didn't reply. Joey didn't really believe he was going to leave, but he never had much to say when Joey talked about going back. Maybe he was serious. But he was too young to retire. And people only left when they retired.

*Or if they stood up when the rocks came.*

As the boys entered the debris field surrounding

the crater, the land sloped up toward the rim. Everywhere was evidence that the area had been mined: concrete anchor points for equipment, smoothed paths through the rubble, and pre-AGLS boot prints.

Joey stumbled over a glassy stone, a near-perfect cube about the size of his boot. He picked it up and stared into its transparent depth. It was heavy like iron. Suspended inside were specs of white, and clouds of browns and purples. He hefted it up to the sunlight, and it seemed to glow.

"This rock is beautiful. It's like all the stars is stuck in it."

Stan looked at the block. "Oh. That's why they call it galaxite. Not a clever name, but it fits."

"They don't mine it?"

"No money in it," Stan said with a shrug. "It's mostly just in the way. We have to dig around it. It's so dense it destroys the grinders. You can't even cut it with a water jet. The laser cutters just make it warm. And we can't sell it for enough to offset the transport cost of big slabs."

Stan laughed.

"Apparently, I paid attention one day."

"Well, maybe you can give it to Mars when you go there. It'll be what every Martian wants in their apartments."

"Good idea. Help me tape one of them to my back so I can carry it a million kilometers."

"Really?"

"No, goofy," Stan laughed.

Joey frowned. He couldn't fathom people not wanting to look at the rock. It reminded him of the tile. It was beautiful to stare into.

"Well, when we get to Mars, I'm going to buy a rocket and come back for all the galaxite that TMS leaves behind."

"Oh. So you're going now."

"No, but if I did, me and my dad will mine the galaxite and you can make pricing tables. And we'll make a bunch of money for our retirement trusts."

Stan scoffed.

"I doubt you'll ever come back to an asteroid after you see a real planet."

"Have you seen one?"

"When I was really young. But mostly I've seen the pictures and video."

"Video?" Joey asked.

"It's like a picture but it moves."

*Someday I'll learn what all the words mean.* But he forgot about galaxite and Mars when they crested the lip of the deep crater.

They were greeted by a pale dome of light flooding the bowl of the two-kilometer-wide crater. Near the rim of the crater the light stopped as if contained by a flattened bubble with iridescent pink fringes.

Twenty meters below them, in the center of the crater, was a village. It was not the precise layout of the miner's village. Instead, dozens of boxy apartments and stacked cargo containers made a warren of narrow alleys branching off a wider main street. Every structure was painted in vibrant red-oranges, yellows, and pale blues. At the end of the main street was a tall building, taller than the Mushroom. It was a grand ramshackle of massive cargo boxes stacked on top of each other. It was painted white with golden-yellow accents. Joey could just make out fluttering banners of every shape and color strung from the top, and down to other buildings.

"Is this the tomb?" Joey said. *No, it can't be.* He opened his notebook to the drawing of the tile. There were only checkmarks on half of the dots. By his estimates, they were not to the tomb yet, not even on the right asteroid. But Stan had said the asteroids should have moved a lot.

"No. We still have several more asteroids to go until we get there. Look."

Stan pointed. A crowd, mostly obscured by the buildings, flowed out of the largest structure.

"Reffies?" Joey said.

# CHAPTER TWENTY-TWO

S tan was puzzled by something. He didn't seem worried that they may be so close to reffies, known eaters of their own dead and raiders of mining colonies. The only thing that kept the reffies at bay was the tireless watch of foremen.

"Must be. But how could reffies have an OxDome?"

"OxDome?"

"That's what that pink bubble is. It's a kind of portable atmosphere. They're quite expensive. They must have stolen one."

Joey turned to a blank page to sketch the village. Stan watched in fascination as the picture formed on the page. Even though he only used the black grease pencil on white paper, Joey captured the faint energy dome by shading the areas around it darker.

"So, they can just walk around in there without suits?" Joey said.

"Yeah."

"Why don't we have one?"

"Because they trap the dust from mining. It just hangs there in the air, or collects on the equipment.

Better to let it settle somewhere else, or fly out into space."

"Who'd reffies steal it from, then?"

Stan shrugged as he studied his computer screen.

"According to my chart, the oxygen well, and hopefully a working recharge station, are on the edge of the village."

"You mean we have to go in?" Joey licked his lips.

"Yeah," Stan said excitedly, "we might get to see a real live reffie."

"I hope not."

"Relax, my understanding is they only eat *their* dead," Stan said, then he added, "Although, a couple dopey kids on their own seems like a reason for a feast. There's always some poor traveling hero who comes across cannibals, and they always lose at least one of their group."

Joey licked his lips again.

"Isn't there another place we can recharge?"

"Not on this rock. Anyway, don't you want to see one?"

"No," Joey said, but his curiosity was raging.

"Come on. There's no one on the outside of the village. We can get really close behind those buildings."

Joey was doubtful as they scrambled down the steep crater wall. They paused at the pink edge of the OxDome.

"Do you think they have claws and fangs and stuff?" Joey said.

"I'll bet they're like big insects or something."

"How do we—"

Stan stepped through without hesitation. The energy membrane flowed around him like liquid, then closed behind him, leaving short-lived concentric ripples. Stan turned back, and motioned for Joey to follow. He excitedly pointed toward his ears.

Joey stepped through. Despite the insulation of the AGLS, he was always aware of the cold vacuum of space. Going into the OxDome was like the warm water jets of his shower passing over him.

The sounds of a crowd hit him, tinny through the AGLS's external microphones. Joey had never experienced sound outside before. He looked at his forearm computer. It indicated he was in an oxygen-rich atmosphere. He flipped open a protective flap on his arm computer. Stan tried to stop him, but Joey pressed the pressure vent button.

There was a rush of air as the pressures of the OxDome and the AGLS equalized. Joey worked his jaw to equalize his ears. The air was not like came from the recharge station, or the sterile air of his apartment. It was dry and tasted like iron and dust.

The sounds of life hit in a confusing onslaught. There were doors opening and closing, metal clanging, and heavy thumps. There was the murmur of people. There was the tiny spit and hiss of the micro thrusters firing. The cacophony was a magical assault. It wasn't pleasant but it was a welcome change from the isolation of a pressure suit. His breathing was no longer the dominant sound, the world was. It sounded open. It sounded unrestricted.

Then he heard singing. Other than occasional work cadences, there wasn't much singing on the colony. Certainly there was nothing like what he heard now.

Different voices sang different parts that flowed in and out of each other. It was a slow chaos of notes that merged into a beautiful, sad chorus. And he had to get closer.

Joey didn't wait to see if Stan followed. He jogged closer to the village. Through narrow gaps between the boxes he glimpsed the crowd. Like a grain of sugar on the tongue, the glimpses were only enough to make him want more. The crowd flowed toward the opposite end of the village, carrying the sad song with them.

Joey followed. He wanted to hear better, so he released the two latches along the ring joint of his helmet. He gave the dome a quarter turn and lifted it off his head, and the singing hit him directly. He swam in the heartache of it. He had never experienced something so powerful. His eyes blurred with tears.

"What the hell are you doing?" Stan said as he caught up to Joey.

"Vent your suit so you can hear," Joey said.

"I can hear just fine," Stan said.

"It's different. I promise."

Stan frowned and hesitated, then vented the suit and scrunched up his nose and eyes.

"Oh, the air in here is awful," he said. "How can people live like this?"

Then Stan heard the singing.

"It's beautiful, isn't it," Joey said, walking with the crowd.

"It's sad," Stan said with a frown as he followed.

They came to the end of a rusted and battered cargo box. It was at the end of the village, where the main street was at its widest. From here they could see across the village to the buildings of the main street. Compared to the clinical white of TMS, the village was alive with color.

The crowd poured out along the main street. Their song repeated and Joey found himself humming along as he recognized the patterns. Stan pulled Joey back behind the cargo box.

"You really want them to taste your butt stew?"

"I want to see."

Joey shook off Stan's grip and peeked around the corner. He got his first glimpse of the people—and they were just people. Joey was disappointed and relieved that they were not some sort of monstrous creatures. Half the crowd wore some form of pressure suit, but none wore the helmets. The rest wore dirty but colorful clothes that looked to Joey to be something like his sleeping clothes. Anyone not in a pressure suit wore a small, boxy pack strapped to their backs.

"What do you think they mine out here?"

"I don't think they mine?"

"Then what do they do?"

"Sell meat to people who want to see alien tombs."

Joey laughed, but he was scared. More scared than being stuck between two asteroids.

Emerging from the crowd, four large men carried what looked to be a rolled-up blanket above their heads. The quilted diamond pattern was dingy with asteroid dust. The men shifted the load and Joey realized there was a person inside the blanket.

"Oh," Stan said, "they're about to eat!" He gagged.

All the joking about eating people died when he was about to be confronted by it.

Joey didn't care, he wanted be closer to the singing, and he wanted to draw the horrific scene. Otherwise, who would believe him? He imagined the people's faces covered in juices as they tore parts of the person away. If he couldn't see clearly, he was going to draw it like that.

He set his glass dome on the ground and pulled out his notebook. As he roughed in the form of the crowd, the song crescendoed, and tears welled in his eyes. Drawing became impossible. So he watched. He experienced. He would have to draw later from memory.

The crowd had their hands in the air now. Joey stepped forward, and stepped again. He had to see it better.

"That'll be close enough, friends," a man's voice said from behind them.

# CHAPTER TWENTY-THREE

J oey and Stan yelped. When they turned, an old man walked toward them, holding his hands wide in a nonthreatening gesture. Stan wasn't convinced. He backed away. But Joey stood staring. It was only the second time he had seen someone with wrinkles so deep.

The man was not tall, barely taller than Stan. Like others in the crowd, he wore a pressure suit but no helmet. The suit was clean but stained and worn from years of service. The soles of the boots were thin and rounded. The ring joints at the wrists had much of their anodized color worn away, and the shell had many frayed holes in the outer layer. Not even Olly let his suit get that old.

There was a pause in the singing; the sudden silence was broken only by the micro thruster firing from Joey's and Stan's AGLS, and from the man's. Nervously, Joey met the man's gaze. Below his kind eyes, recent tears had cleaned tracks through the coating of dirt. Joey glanced over to the crowd. Someone was speaking now, but the voice did not carry.

"What are they doing?" Joey asked.

"It's a funeral," the old man said. "Please do not disturb it."

*Everyone knows words I don't.*

"What is that?" Joey said, hoping the answer wasn't related to cooking.

The old man gave Joey an understanding smile.

"It's a ceremony for when someone dies," he said.

Joey nodded. He looked at Stan. The older boy was a statue, with his eyes fixed on the old man like he expected to be attacked.

The sad song erupted again and Joey wanted it sung at his funeral, and his dad's, and Stan's. Everyone's.

A tear rolled down the old man's cheek as he looked back toward the funeral. He sung silently. Joey's throat was thick with emotion.

The OxDome started to hum. Their ears plugged as the dome throbbed outward, growing larger in pulses. When it stopped, the edge of the energy field was now ten meters farther out, revealing a patch of ground surrounded by a perimeter of rocks. The throbbing subsided.

The procession moved toward the rocks. The men lowered the body into an open pit, and more people stepped forward and shoveled dirt over it. Joey looked to Stan but there were no answers in his confused face. The old man chuckled.

"She was too old to eat," the old man said. "Meat's too dry."

Stan choked and began coughing. The old man let out a warm laugh. Joey laughed and patted Stan on the shoulder. The old man gave Stan a compassionate smile.

"Sorry for the gallows humor, kid. Don't believe everything you're told."

"Well, what have you got here, Orbison?" a tall woman said as she walked up.

"Couple lads out for a nice stroll," the old man said.

Joey gawped. She was beautiful. Like nothing he had ever seen. The woman's face was lined with fine wrinkles, and she too had tear streaks that cut through the dust on her cheeks. But under the grime, her lips were full and the curves of her face were soft. Joey looked at Stan and saw only distrust in his eyes.

Joey's eyes were drawn back to her. He had never seen a woman, and he didn't understand what he saw. She was utterly alien to him, and yet as familiar as anything. What he felt as he looked her up and down was even more confusing. Her clothes were loose-fitting quilted layers with occasional tighter bands ringed with micro thrusters. The thrusters were fed by hoses that ran along her sides to the same boxy pack he had seen on others. The clothes might have been the same cream as Joey's sleep clothes once, but they were all the colors of asteroid dust now.

The woman looked at the two boys, appraising them. Her eyes lingered on Joey. There was a touch of sadness in them. *The funeral, maybe,* Joey thought. He smiled at her, and she smiled back. Her smile dropped as she turned a hard gaze on Stan.

"Taking your pet for a walk," the woman said.

"Hey!" Stan snapped. "Don't talk about Joey like that."

The woman smirked.

"Oh, you think I was denigrating him, do ya? The pet is the innocent in the equation here, friend."

"Joey, we need to go," Stan said. He had looked scared earlier. Now he seemed to be on the verge of panic.

"I don't know what the two of you are up to," the woman said, "but you're welcome to recharge your suits. I even have some food if you need it."

She held out something wrapped in a cloth. Joey's stomach growled. He hesitated, his mind filled with what body parts might fit in the fist-sized bundle. *Maybe a fist?*

He reached for the bundle and unwrapped it like a rat might leap out. It was a slice of irregular-shaped bread and a chunk of cheese. Joey showed it to Stan. The older boy made no move to remove his helmet.

Joey lifted the food to take a timid bite, but as soon as the smell of fresh bread hit his nostrils, he ate greedily. Biting the cheese and the bread together made him smile so broadly he could hardly keep his mouth closed while chewing.

"When he finishes, kindly get the fuck out," the woman said, focused on Stan. "We don't need to have whoever might be out looking for you find you here. They will not assume anything good about our intentions. They'll just use it as more agitprop."

"Who are you?" Stan said.

"We are refugees," she said. "Sorry. Reffies. Defectors. Castaways. We are Olly. Whatever you want to call us. Just move on. The recharger is over there."

The woman pointed the way to the recharge station.

Joey finished the bread and was trying to swallow the last of the cheese when he picked up his helmet. He tried to brush out the base of his suit's neck hole and moisture collectors. He didn't want to have bread crumbs floating in front of his face for the next couple days. With his helmet under his arm he walked to the recharge station.

Stan hesitated, then walked. The old man and the woman followed. Their gaze never left the boys.

As Stan had figured, the recharge station was old. It was smaller than the unit at the colony. The insulating blankets were torn in places, revealing the layers of Mylar and hex mesh inside.

Singing erupted again from the funeral. It struck Joey at that moment that when Felix died, there was nothing. No songs were sung. No burial of the body by his friends. Other than the scraps of conversation he overheard, Felix was just gone. Like a page torn out of his notebook. The only thing left was the thin strip of paper caught in the spiral binding to remind him the page had been there. Someday that piece would fall out too. It would be as if Felix had never existed.

Stan closed the vents of his suit and connected the one functioning hose. He never took his eyes off the two reffies. As the rush of air fogged the inside of his dome, Stan darted his eyes around nervously.

Joey stepped up to the hose. Before he replaced the glass dome that would silence the sounds of the village, he turned back to the beautiful woman and the old man. The villagers. He decided they were villagers now. He would not call them reffies anymore.

"My name is Joey...Joseph Junior," Joey said. "Can I hear your names?"

The woman raised an eyebrow. It was brief, barely noticeable.

"Arabelle," the woman said.

"Orbison," the old man said.

"Can I ask who died?" Joey said.

Arabelle swallowed hard. It took her a moment to speak.

"Her name was Elizabeth Westing," Arabelle said. "She was a dear friend who loved reading."

"She was also my dear friend. She loved painting the building in the village and making it colorful," Orbison said, his voice shaking. He smiled as a tear slipped from his eye.

"I'm sorry. Thank you for your help," Joey said.

Joey lowered the dome over his head, flipped the latches, and closed his vents. He plugged the hose into his suit. The rush of air was cool and musty. It filled his mind with memories he could not place.

When the fog cleared from Joey's dome, Orbison bowed his head and walked away. Arabelle smiled at him.

"Now," she said, "please. Joey, you can't stay now, not with him here. But come back if you can. You will be welcomed."

She turned a pointed gaze at Stan again. "Go, before we reffies get the reputation as kidnappers of slave masters and their pets."

"What?" Joey said. He was lost. But the tension between Arabelle and Stan swelled.

"Ask him," Arabelle said, pointing at Stan. "Oh,

and watch for the dark ships cruising around here. They're slave traders looking for people from our village, or yours. I promise you they are not as nice as your current masters. Either of you."

"I think we saw one," Joey said. *Please, I want to stay.* "It was boxy. It was old and rusty looking. Stan said it was an old troop ship."

"That's it," she said and held up her hand to stop any further conversation. "You must go now."

Joey wanted more time with them. He wanted to learn about their lives. He wanted his dad to meet them.

As they headed out of the village, Joey watched as the last shovelfuls of dirt were thrown on the grave. He could see now that there were many graves, each with a block of stone at the head. Two men carried a new block of stone forward and placed it at the head of the freshly filled pit. Elizabeth Westing was roughly chiseled into one side. Evidence this woman had existed would last for years. *Maybe a thousand years, like the fancy people in the tomb.* Felix had been erased from The Mining Society, and a refugee who liked reading and painting would be remembered. *Someone dying should mean something,* Joey thought. *They should be remembered.*

The crowd turned back toward the village and broke into song again. It was thin through the AGLS speakers, but this song was a celebration. A celebration of Elizabeth Westing. It was a raucous melody that filled Joey with as much joy as the other song had filled him with sadness. He tried to make out the words but could not. But the melody was a permanent fixture in his memory until the end of his days. He hummed it softly to himself, not wanting it to carry over ShortComs.

At the edge of the pink OxDome membrane, Joey turned to wave to Arabelle, but she was not there. He thought he saw her merging with the lively procession but he could not be sure. He wanted to see her again, and Orbison too. But they would not be at TMS when he got back.

Joey pushed through the OxDome membrane and the world was silent again.

Cold again.

# CHAPTER TWENTY-FOUR

Joesph Senior slid the inner door of his apartment open, slamming it against the stops. He ignored the blaring buzzer as he stomped to the cramped couch, sat, stood back up, paced a couple times, and sat back down. He rubbed his face.

"If I had my pickaxe, I would have put it in his chest," Joseph said, his voice shaking with anger. "I never felt nothing like that."

Hagen sighed as he slid the airlock door closed. He had to shut it twice to silence the buzzer.

"You know, we all despise Michael," Hagen said. "He reports every little violation he spots. And we're pretty sure he makes a lot of it up. And what he gets out of it is so stupid. A pat on the back, an extra dessert here and there. A feeling of power over people. I don't really know. Maybe it's just boredom."

Joseph seethed; he didn't want to talk about Michael.

"Are you seriously telling me you haven't found any trace of the boys?"

"Officially, no," Hagen said. "The governor wants

to control the information about this."

"Why? Two boys wandered off," Joseph Senior said. "What needs to be controlled about that?"

"They don't tell me much more than they tell the miners."

"But you do know more?"

Hagen hesitated.

"Damn it, Hagen," Joseph said, his exasperation getting the best of him. "Why won't they tell me? Is Joey dead?"

The question came out with a sudden spluttering cry. A noise he had never heard himself make. He had not cried since he was a boy, and that was so long ago he didn't even remember what made him upset.

Hagen let out a long sigh.

"We don't know."

"You said you could search the whole rock in a couple hours. That was two days ago."

"Look, as we both figured, the boys went out in the field. They went south of the dig site. By the footprints, it looked like they were walking together, probably goofing off. But then they just stop."

"What does that mean?"

"It looks like they jumped off the asteroid."

Joseph laughed at the absurdity of that idea.

"We can't even throw a small rock off the asteroid. How could they jump?"

"It is possible. But very dangerous. You know, working up in the Mushroom has given me a lot of time around the governor and Stan. Stan is...He's a smart kid. Spoiled. Get this, he breaks into his dad's study all the time. His dad knocks him around and they rework the security. But he gets in again and makes it obvious he did. It was him who disabled the alert for the recharge station. He put his name in the logs."

"Okay, but what about Joey? Where did they go? Can you take me?"

"I don't think that's a good idea, Joseph."

"I don't care what's a good idea. I care about Joey."

Hagen chuckled.

"Why are you laughing at me?"

"Not at you. I wouldn't laugh at you, Joseph. You are the most sincere man I've ever known. I'm laughing at the situation."

Joseph frowned. He wished they could just get to the part where Joey was back home with him.

"I can't take you to see where they went," Hagen continued. "I don't want to be forced to retire before I'm funded. I can, however, tell you how to get there. And I can tell you a feature of your suit that will explain how they might have gotten off the rock."

*Our three days are ours,* Joseph thought.

# CHAPTER TWENTY-FIVE

Joey and Stan made two more jumps that morning. And with all that was swimming around in Joey's head, the excitement and terror he had felt before barely registered.

Joey trailed behind Stan as they walked in silence. Stan was distant and pensive. Joey wasn't eager to talk either. There was too much to process. He kept replaying the conversation with Arabelle in his mind. Yet another person with more knowledge them him, more words than him.

One thing he was sure of, everything they had been told about the reffies was a lie. *Villagers*, he reminded himself. Maybe there were some as bad as the stories, but the stories said they were all bad. So bad that the foremen stood around the perimeter of the dig sites in case they were attacked. *But not so bad that the foremen needed to guard the camp at night? Then why were they standing there day after day, rifles ready? Ready for what?*

Maybe the real fight with the reffies happened away from the colony. It was only a couple days ago they had heard about a raid that was prevented. They were stopped before they could get close. Maybe the foremen around the crater were the last line of defense. And really, what did he know about the villagers anyway? He only talked to two of them, and didn't see anything, really. Just another thing he did not know.

Despite his scattered mind, one thing was always there. Joey couldn't escape the vision of Arabelle. Seeing a woman for the first time brought into focus the all-male life of a colony miner. He didn't know what to do with what he felt. He didn't even know there were such feelings before, and his stomach was in knots. He felt warm inside, and nervous, and happy, and sad. She was the most beautiful thing he had ever seen.

She had a way about her, calm and commanding. Some of the foremen had that too. Not the mean ones like Ganyon, but others: Alejo, Hagen, who he remembered his dad talking to when he was younger.

*She said I could come back. That I would be welcomed.*

A sound cut through ShortComs. It was only loud enough to trigger the coms briefly. Joey looked around. It came again. He smiled.

"Are you singing?" Joey said.

"Yeah," Stan said with an embarrassed laugh. "The song is stuck in my head. Repeating over and over."

"Isn't it great?"

Stan looked back over his shoulder. He was embarrassed.

"Yeah. It is great."

He started singing the melody.

"Oh, I think you got one part wrong," Joey said and sang what he thought was the correct melody.

"Hey, you're right," Stan said and sang the correct version.

Joey joined in and they passed the next twenty minutes singing the song in unison. The beat infected their walks. They were practically dancing. They took turns singing parts, discovering the call-and-response singing of generations gone long before them.

And when the next jump came, Joey found himself in higher spirits. Maybe Stan was right, this was the good part of this insane trip. Spending time with his friend.

A friend who had to answer a few questions.

# CHAPTER TWENTY-SIX

S tan's computer led the boys into a field of great curving flakes of rock peeled up from the ground like frozen cresting waves. Joey traced his gloved fingers along the edges. As the flakes grew more dense, the beauty of the formations gave way to frustration. Joey and Stan climbed over, around, and under the flakes, taking care not to snag their suits.

After a time the formations thinned, and the ground started to level, and then ended all together. They stood on the lip of the biggest crater Joey had ever seen. The wall swept away from them in either direction, and met again in the distance. The far side was lost in the shadow of another asteroid, but it was clear that something broke the crater wall up in a way that looked too regular to be natural.

"The other side is a couple kilometers away," Stan said.

"Okay, let's go," Joey said and stomped his heel.

"I think maybe we should go around."

"Won't that take longer?"

"Yeah. Another few hours at least."

"So let's jump. I bet we make it across in three jumps."

Stan looked over the edge. Directly below, the bottom was swallowed in shadow. He licked his lips.

"Yeah," Stan said.

"Is the jump making you nervous?"

"Stupid, isn't it?"

"Really stupid."

"Okay," Stan said with a sigh, "I don't think we should do so many jumps though. We'd use to much HTP. Let's jump down, then walk the rest of the way."

"Okay."

Stan stomped his heel, then the boys leapt out from the edge in a low arc. They weren't going to make it past the shadow. Landing in the dark made Joey's stomach flutter in a way he hadn't felt since yesterday's jumps. But the landing was uneventful.

He swept his eyes around. Down in the bowl of the crater, the wall towered over them. They could easily make that jump, but it still felt confining. Only slight ripples and occasional cracks broke up the smooth plain of dark rock between them and the next jump.

Joey took the first step forward and Stan didn't immediately follow. And when he passed into the direct sunlight he saw why. His white Angel suit glowed against the near-black rock. Stan checked the chart on his arm computer. He pointed across the field.

"We have to go straight across," Stan said, still hesitating. After scanning the sky for a long moment, he set his jaw and started forward.

"I want to run," Joey said, looking back over his shoulder.

"Me too. But it would use too much oxygen. We are well past any mining operations for this cluster; this is it for supplies. Watch the sky while I navigate."

"Okay."

They fell into a silent march across the plain. Joey scanned the sky in methodical sweeps. The creaks and hum of his AGLS, and the little pulses of micro thrusters, grew louder and louder in his ears. Even though he would never hear the dark ship, he imagined the cacophony of the suit drowning out its approach. Sweat beaded on his upper lip and brow.

"Do you know who makes the comic books?" Joey said, desperate to distract himself.

"What?" Stan said after a long silence, as if it just dawned on him that Joey was speaking.

"The comic books. Do you know who draws them?"

"They are done by a company on Mars."

"If I went there could I see how they make them?"

"I thought you were going back to TMS."

"Well, yeah, but I want to know how they make the lincs. You know how they get them so black?"

"I've never read them. My dad said comics are for…" Stan trailed off.

"What?"

"Nothing. I just started thinking I hope this tomb is worth it," Stan said.

"What do you mean?"

"I mean it's been fun running around with you. But we could have done that closer to home, you know. Without the danger."

"I don't know. A thousand-year-old tomb. That might not be human."

"Yeah. That would be neat."

"And you figured out how to jump to another asteroid. I bet Tom from your book never did that."

Stan beamed with pride.

"That was pretty awesome."

They walked on, their goal never seeming to get closer.

"His name was Felix," Joey said after a while. "He was my dad's friend, and he was always nice to me."

"What?" Stan said, confused.

"Felix was the miner who was killed by the Trojans a couple days ago."

"Okay," Stan said. "An Olly, right?"

"We're all a little Olly, remember. His name was Felix. He was my dad's friend, and he was always nice to me. Your turn."

"His name was Felix...I'm not doing a reffie ritual."

"Why don't miners get tombs? Or funerals?"

Stan didn't answer for a long moment. Joey looked at him. Stan's eyes were furtive, looking anywhere but at Joey.

"It's hard to explain."

Joey laughed. He stopped and made a sweeping gesture around the lava field. Stan looked around, still not meeting Joey's eyes.

"What else are we going to do?" Joey said.

"I guess it's just not in our traditions."

"Well, the aliens get tombs," Joey said as he started walking again. "The villagers get a rock with their name on it, and they get singing. I want singing. When we get back I'm going to teach people to sing, and we're going to sing for Felix. Then we'll all say something we liked about him."

"Boy, you're going to be eating ear with noodles soon," Stan said.

Joey laughed but it faded. They had reached a point where the end of the field looked as far away as the beginning, and both looked unreachable. Without realizing, they had both started walking quicker. The fear of the dark ship had them almost giddy.

"When we get back," Stan said, "I'm going to stay inside for a month."

They forced themselves to slow only to find that they were half walking, half running again.

"You know, sometimes it seems like you don't want to answer my questions."

"Sorry. My mind is elsewhere a lot of the time."

"Like just now."

"Look!" Stan said, and pointed.

In the distance, black faceted spires of rock stabbed twenty meters up from a low area in the crater wall. The asteroid that had put the area in shadow had moved along. Sunlight flashed off the facets and seemed to illuminate the inside of the spires, making them glow dully against the black sky. Joey had spent his entire life around asteroid terrain, the jagged and smooth, the hard and soft, the angled and rounded. He had never seen something as geometrically clean as this formation. Nothing other than equipment brought there by men. Nothing except the tile that sent them on this mad journey.

There were dozens of six-sided columns that shot straight up, then tapered to chisel points at the head, and stood in a line like a great wall. The wall ran at least a hundred meters along the edge of the plain. The last spires on either end were shattered, great chunks ripped from them by some collision long ago.

They arrived to the base of the wall tired. The anxiety of being so exposed had them panting as if they had been running. Joey calmed his breathing and walked right up the face of the nearest column. He ran his hand along the pitted surface, wiping away dust and revealing them to be galaxite. Sunlight scattered inside it, split into a thousand diffused beams by the heavily pitted surface.

"Someone built this?" he said.

"I don't know, but it doesn't look natural," Stan said.

"Maybe the someone made galaxite too," Joey said as he walked for the end of the wall, dragging his hand along it the whole way. Bathed in the dull glow, he tried to imagine what it would look like cleaned of dust and free of the pitting.

"Maybe. I wonder how long it has been here," Stan said.

"A thousand years." Joey shrugged.

They reached the ruined end of the wall and clambered over rubble to see what was behind it. Any clue to what the wall had been part of was a crater now. Like so many things in Joey's life lately, the ruins raised more questions than answers. If he were a good miner he would have kept his small tank of knowledge full. Instead, he let the tank grow so big it could never be filled. *Olly must have had the biggest tank of them all before me.* Joey chuckled to himself.

"What are you laughing at?" Stan said.

"I was thinking they'll change Olly's name in The

Book to Joey," he said as he jumped down to the edge of the crater, his feet kicking up motes of fine black dust.

Stan laughed as he jumped down, and the motes ballooned into a cloud. The dust danced around their legs, then was puffed away by the AGLS dust-repellent system. With no atmosphere, the dust settled quickly, only to be kicked up again with the slightest shuffle of their feet.

Stan pointed to a bright sunlit asteroid in the sky.

"There it is. The penultimate asteroid."

"The what?"

"The jump before the last one. Unless you think you've had enough."

"Not even close," Joey said.

"Okay. I figure we could go off this big thing."

Stan patted one of the broken columns. It lay like a dimly lit ramp to the sky. They only needed to run for the end and jump. They had done it so many times now, but it still got Joey's heartbeat up, and his palms sweaty. And now that they were so close, it was like the end of a shift at the crater. A couple more big swings and the day would be done. A couple more jumps and it would be time to go home.

He felt his breath quicken. He had that air-starved suit feeling. It was so bad he had to check that he still had air. The levels were good. He reminded himself to trust the suit. The alarms would go off if anything was amiss.

Stan climbed the fallen spire.

"Stop!" Joey said in an urgent whisper. "They're coming."

# CHAPTER TWENTY-SEVEN

S tan looked back. Joey pointed low in the sky. The dark ship was streaking right for them. Right for the bright white suits like they were beacons. Stan jumped down, and they crouched in the swirling dust behind the fallen column.

Where could they go? The best they could do would be to go back to the other side of the wall, and that would only buy them minutes. The ship ripped by overhead and disappeared beyond the wall. It appeared again far away, attitude rockets spitting out in different directions as it made a wide circle to come back around.

"Run," Joey shouted.

They ran, stumbling over the broken ground between crater and wall, and leaving a trail of the fine black dust floating behind them. They made it halfway along the wall when the ship came over the top. It was already banking hard in a wide arc to try and cut them off. With no other options, they ran back the way they came and into the plumes of black dust. It was too dense to risk running. They were wasting oxygen, and their white suits would always lead the ship right to them.

"We have to make the jump," Joey said.

"They will see us!"

Joey looked at the cloud dissipating from around them.

"Turn off your dust-repellent system," he said.

"Are you insane?"

Joey flipped up the small cover on his forearm computer, the cover for the buttons you should not use out in the field, and pressed a small red triangle. He stomped around in a circle, and the black cloud billowed and clung to everything. Before long he was nearly covered. Stan followed his lead. They picked up handfuls of the dust and threw it at each other.

"This is so Olly," Joey said, laughing. He could not tell if he was having fun, or if he was giddy from the terror.

"Should I press it?" Stan asked, pointing at the ELT.

"No. We're so close."

Joey didn't wait for a protest. He scrambled out of the cloud and up the fallen tower of rock. The black dust had worked into the ring joints of his suit, stiffening them, and he felt the grit with each movement. *Even something that looks soft will destroy your suit out here.*

The ship arced overhead, finally getting its wild turns under control. There was no way to tell if they were spotted, but the ship settled into circling, only thirty meters away.

"Come on. It's working," Joey said, holding out his hand to pull Stan up.

Stan hesitated, then grabbed Joey's hand and

climbed. It was twenty meters to the broken end of the rock. The micro thrusters were quickly blasting the dust off parts of their suits, the white starting to shine through. Joey stomped his heel. He ran for all his worth and jumped. He didn't even know if Stan was behind him.

Joey streaked out into space. Despite his terror he was breathing free again. He looked down. Stan was below him. Their Angel shells were nearly blasted clean.

Below them, the dark ship settled on the surface, kicking up a massive cloud of black dust. In a pulse, the dust blasted away from the ship and a hatch folded open from the side. Several men came out wearing armored pressure suits and carrying rifles. Before long the boys were too high to see what the men were doing. And when the gravity of the next asteroid caught them, and the micro thruster flipped them around, the ship was all they could make out down on the dark surface.

Joey craned his neck to look back, but he was falling now and that demanded his attention.

# CHAPTER TWENTY-EIGHT

"Turn it on," Joseph Senior growled at Foreman Alejo. He thrust the handle of his pickaxe at the recharge station. It had taken ten minutes to walk here from the mess hall, and he had walked fast. If he was lucky, he had fifteen minutes of air before he got desperate.

Alejo's eyes were pleading with Joseph, when they weren't glancing around at the crowd. Alejo held his rifle across his chest, finger laid straight along the frame above the trigger.

The agitated crowd of miners encircling the recharge station had gone silent. No miner had ever barked an order at a foreman that they had heard. They didn't know what the consequences would be. Before Joseph had roused them in the mess hall ten minutes ago, they had never thought to think about such a thing. Sure, Ganyon was aggressive, and so were a couple other foremen. But most of the time, when a miner caught their eye they deserved it.

"I can't do it, Joseph," Alejo said.

"I saw their boot prints heading south of the crater," Joseph said, seeing no reason to drag Hagen into this. "We are going to find them."

"All of you?" Alejo said.

"Yeah, we'll treat it like a dig. Each man will be responsible for a section."

"It's a good plan but a bad idea. I can't."

Joseph Senior took a step toward Alejo. The foreman licked his lips, glancing down at the pickaxe gripped in Joseph's hand. The miners looked to each other, hoping for a clue about what to do next. Joseph Senior knew what was coming. The recharge pumps were going to be turned on, whatever steps in between might come. He was losing some of the crowd, but he did not notice, and he did not care.

"Open the panel or get out of the way," Joseph snarled and stepped forward again. A couple of the miners backed away.

"This will be bad for both of us."

"I don't care about that. I care about finding those boys."

"I do too," Alejo said, looking desperate.

"Then turn it on," someone in the crowd snapped. Half the crowd surged forward. Alejo's finger edged toward the trigger. Joseph Senior held up a hand and the crowd stopped.

"What's going on here, Alejo?" Governor Emerson said.

Using the flat side of his rifle, Foreman Ganyon shoved miners aside, clearing a path for the governor. Striding through the parting crowd, the governor scowled.

"They want me to turn on the pumps," Alejo said.

A few miners voiced their agreement; the rest

played it safe or backed down completely. Joesph hardly moved.

"I've never seen a whole flock of Ollys," Ganyon said.

The governor held up a hand to silence Ganyon.

"Why do you want the pumps turned on, Joseph?"

"We are going to find the boys."

"Being a father at TMS is about making the future generation of miners. About making Oscars. Your father did it, but you have not."

"Say what you want about me, or Joey," Joseph said, "but we're going. For your son as well as mine."

"No you're not. We've already potentially lost one resource, we're not going to risk you too."

Joseph grimaced. *My son is more than a resource.*

"Our three days are ours," Joseph said. "Chapter one."

Using his son's argument against the governor now made Joseph chuckle.

"That is not what it is about," the governor said.

"It's pretty plain words," someone in the crowd said.

The miners murmured and nodded in agreement. The governor opened his mouth to speak—

"Yeah, Governor," another said, "this is how we're gonna spend *our* three days."

"Right. Plus the extra one you said we get on account of the dig being called early."

"Turn it on, Alejo," Joseph said.

Alejo looked to the governor, and found no answers. The crowd was getting louder.

Ganyon surged toward Joseph, his rifle half-raised.

"You're worth more to the Society than three Joeys," Ganyon said.

"Ganyon, quiet," the governor snapped. "Joseph, you have to let the experts track him."

"What have the experts found so far?" Joseph said.

The governor didn't respond. He watched the miners growing more agitated.

"That Joey found some sort of alien artifact," Joseph said, "and he's on his way to find more, and that Stan planned the whole thing? That they jumped off the asteroid?"

The miners buzzed with confusion.

"Turn it on, Alejo."

Joseph took a another step toward Alejo.

"Don't you turn on that fucking machine," Ganyon shouted.

Alejo's eyes darted from Joseph to Foreman Ganyon. Joseph stepped closer.

"Not another step, Joseph," Ganyon snarled.

Alejo lowered his rifle and stepped away from the recharge station. Joseph Senior stepped up to the side of the station.

"That's enough," Ganyon shouted, shoving the barrel of his rifle against the dome of Joseph's helmet.

Joseph turned in time to see a brief flash of green light explode Ganyon's head in a cloud of bloody mist. Gore jetted up, propelled by the air escaping the ruptured dome. Ganyon's body sank to the ground, micro thrusters misfiring and sending one of his arms flipping back and forth. Blood filled the remaining bowl of the fused-quartz dome and spilled over the melted rim into a freezing puddle in the regolith.

Joseph looked around wildly, trying to figure out what happened. He saw Alejo, frozen in shock, with his rifle still aimed were Ganyon had been.

The miners and the governor were stunned into inaction.

Alejo let his rifle drop onto its sling. He put a hand on Joseph's shoulder.

"It's okay, Joseph," he said, "I got it."

Alejo turned the pumps on, and Joseph connected the hose. When the fog in his helmet faded he saw the governor staring at him. *I guess you're not controlling the information now, sir.*

More foremen were arriving and the miners had all lost their nerve. The foremen stared at the body of Ganyon. The governor stood there, seeming to mumble to himself, eyes darting. They were all in shock and Joseph wasn't going to wait to see what would happen with they got hold of themselves.

Joseph reached down and grabbed Ganyon's rifle, pulling at the sling still looped around his arm. This seemed to wake the other foreman up. Joseph got the sling free. In the confusion, foremen raised their rifles, only to have their aim blocked by other foremen who made a grab for Joseph.

Joseph spun around, stomped his left heel, ran, and jumped out over the rim of the crater. He screamed as the micro thrusters shot him in a high arc. Hot rifle fire flashed past him and fizzled out in the cold of space. He landed, tumbling hard to the ground a kilometer away, well south of the dig site. He didn't wait to see if anyone followed. He stomped his heel and jumped again.

A couple more jumps and he should be close to where Hagen said Joey went.

# CHAPTER TWENTY-NINE

Joey stumbled to his feet, trying to slow his breathing. Previous jumps had been all about the dizzying sensory overload. This jump had been about the slave traders. Escaping them. The micro thrusters rocketing him up, flipping him around, and letting him fall again, were all overshadowed.

He looked back toward the other asteroid, back toward the rusting hulk of a ship. It was too far away to see any sign of it. There was no way to know if they had escaped capture again. But for now, at least, they weren't being chased.

Joey's nose wrinkled. Two days of running and sweating added up, and the waste systems were near capacity. It was starting to stink inside his AGLS. His skin was sticky, and all the straps chafed. Parts of his skin were raw from friction in places he never gave a thought to before.

He reactivated the dust-repellent systems. At least he could do something about that. Clouds of dust leapt away from the shell of his suit. He worked his joints trying to free any trapped particles. Even after that, the stainless steel ring joints were still gritty as they slid against each other. *In space you take care of your equipment*, Joey thought with a rueful laugh.

Stan sat up and just stared back toward where the slave traders would be. His mouth hung slightly open, and he kept blinking over and over.

"What would I do on Mars?" Joey said.

"What?" Stan asked after a long pause.

"If I went there, what would I do? Could I draw the Olly comic books?"

Stan was slow to respond like he was waking from a long nap.

"You would leave your dad?"

"No," Joey said. "When the Earth-Mars people get here I can tell them we gotta get my dad too."

"That won't work," Stan said.

"Why not?"

Stan looked at Joey for a long time. He lowered his gaze.

"I know Mars was my idea," Stan said, "but I think it's time to go back."

"What? No way. We have one more jump, and it's a small one." Joey pointed at the small asteroid on the horizon behind them. "That's it, right?"

"It is. But I want to go home. I don't want to run anymore."

"That's what you wanted."

"I really just wanted us to have fun. And we did. We had fun, right?"

"Why can't we have more fun? On Mars."

"I...I honestly didn't think we'd get this far. I thought we'd make the first jump and get caught."

Joey scowled.

"How come you never answer my questions?"

"I do."

"Okay. Tell me why I can't get my dad."

"You just can't."

"That ain't an answer."

Stan didn't reply.

"What did Arabelle mean when she called me a pet?"

"Nothing, she was just being mean."

"To who?"

"*To whom.* I don't know."

"I don't believe you. Arabelle said the people in the ship were slave traders. She said they would not be as nice as my current masters. What are current masters?"

"We're friends, right?"

"Yeah, but that's not an answer."

"If we didn't make it to Mars we'd still be friends."

"I guess. What are current masters? What's a slave?"

Stan was quiet.

"She told me to ask you," Joey said. When Stan didn't answer, Joey shouted, "What is it?"

"I just want us to be friends. Wherever we are."

Joey stood up and loomed over Stan.

"Tell me," he said.

"I don't care about—"

"Tell me. Tell me. Tell me." Joey got closer and louder with every word.

Stan sighed. He could not look at Joey.

"A slave is someone who is owned by someone

else, owned by a master, and he must do work for them."

Joey frowned. *How does someone own someone?*

"What, like a tool?"

Stan shrugged, still unwilling to look at Joey.

"Am I a slave?"

"No." Stan was indignant. "You only have to work four days a week. You get to vote for governors. Slaves don't get any of that. Plus, all the miners get money paid through their retirement trust."

"Okay, you can go back. You can tell the governor that me and my dad are retiring."

"You can't. TMS decides when you retire."

"But I want to retire now."

Again, Stan said nothing.

"Arabelle was right. I'm a pet. I'm owned like a pet or a tool. Like I own my pickaxe." Joey panted for air.

"You're not my pet. You're my friend. Anyway, who cares what Arabelle says. She is a reffie savage."

"You take that back. She's not a savage. She's better than you or your stupid dad. She said I could come to the village. Would you let me go there, *master*?"

"No."

Stan's head sank. The dome of his suit rested on his knees. Joey stared at him. Stan was shaking.

"I am sorry," Stan said without looking up. "It will all be better when we're back at TMS, friend."

"Friend? How can I be friends with someone who owns me? I never want—"

Joey cut off. The aluminized tape was peeled off the ELT on Stan's belt, and the protective flap was up, exposing a red dome-shaped button.

"Don't you dare push that button," Joey said.

Stan did not reply.

"Stan?"

Joey watched for the slightest movement.

"Stan?"

Stan shifted, and Joey pounced and flattened him against the ground. He pinned Stan's arms down. But Stan bucked and rolled on top of Joey. Stan couldn't keep his hold. Swinging a pickaxe all day hardened Joey's muscles, and his rage made him savage. They rolled, and the crunch of rocks and regolith against the suit echoed in Joey's helmet.

Stan wedged his feet under Joey's stomach and shoved. Joey went flying back and the crash of his life-support pack stung his ears. Then he heard a voice he hadn't heard since school.

"*Leak Detected. Leak Detected. Leak Detected,*" the suit's warning system said, its dire warnings delivered by a dispassionate artificial voice. They called her Bitching Betty. Joey laughed a sour laugh to himself. Before meeting Arabelle, the higher pitch of the voice felt alien to him. Now he realized it was the voice of someone like Arabelle.

It was a small leak or he'd be dead, but unless a sensor was damaged, he definitely had one.

"Please don't push it, Stan," Joey pleaded.

"I already pushed it. Before the jump," Stan said, his helmet still resting on his knees.

# CHAPTER THIRTY

Joseph flew, arcing over a low ridge, micro thrusters controlling his descent. He landed in a run, easing the impact. He felt something he had only felt twice since he was a child. Making the huge leaps with the AGLS jump system—once he got the hang of it—filled him with joy. The satisfaction of hard work and duty were what he thrived on. He had fun with his friends. But joy wasn't part of a miner's life. All *according to The Book?*

The other time he felt joy was when he had been given a child to raise.

The joy of the jump faded as Joseph noticed he was standing among child-sized boot prints in the regolith. Scattered around were the prints of the foreman who had been searching for the boys. He traced the boys' prints leading back the way he'd come. The sky above the ridge was empty. Expecting foremen, he stared for a long moment, then scanned the horizon in all directions. There were no foremen in sight.

As the adrenaline subsided, guilt flooded through him as if he had pulled the trigger that ended Foreman

Ganyon. *Didn't you set all this in motion?* He had never liked Ganyon, and the foreman's death left Joseph conflicted. The was no way of knowing if Ganyon was about to shoot him. *Oscar would be safe rather than sorry.* Joseph let out a rueful laugh. *What the hell does Oscar and Olly have to do with any of this?*

It was strange to him that the note Joey had left, misquoted from The Book, was the loose thread on a knitted undershirt. *Our three days are ours.* The sentiment was right: a miner's three-day break was his to enjoy, and reflect.

Joseph followed the prints to a sharp drop-off. At the edge, they simply stopped. They were not clean prints—they were the prints of someone running, jumping. He looked out over the edge, down into the dizzying abyss. RN-3b was not there now, but he guessed it would be in about thirty minutes. He scanned the sky, looking for any sign of them, hoping he didn't see them.

Was his boy even still alive? Had they made it to RN-3b? Or did their trip end with that first jump, and now the boys were drifting out into the void and running out of oxygen, destined to be just another speck of debris in the vast emptiness.

His thoughts turned morbid and strangely clinical, perhaps to cope. He imagined their little frozen bodies would never be found once their temperature equalized with the vacuum. Maybe one day they would be caught by the gravity of some planet or asteroid, or the sun. Joseph hoped that if they were truly lost, someday, even if a million years from now, they would fall to Earth and be seen as a meteorite by someone. And that the sight would be something special for them.

Joseph had worried Joey would struggle as a miner. But the boy's output had been proving him wrong. Joseph himself had struggled at first, but his dad had helped him through it. *I failed you, Joey.*

But Joey was an Olly. In the truest sense. Joseph knew in his heart Joey was built different. And if Olly was like Joey, then being an Olly must be damned good. Joseph looked down at the rifle still in his hands. *Everything I've done will cost me dearly.*

Joseph had seen Felix stand up when the rocks came. It wasn't an accident. It couldn't have been. He had said nothing to anyone, because no one ever talked about the rare deaths. It was a private thing, his dad had said. Joseph had planned on saying the same thing to Joey after Felix's death. But when he opened his mouth to speak, his throat got thick with emotion. He kept it a private thing. Anyway, every death was always the miner's fault. They were always an Olly, and that's why they died. *Or maybe that was just controlled information.*

Would Joey have one day done the same thing, stand in the path of an asteroid, or jump into space to become a moonlet? There was no Olly story where he purposely let himself die. But maybe now they'd add one to The Book.

Eventually, he would have to go back. He wasn't sure if he did anything wrong exactly. Like Joey's insane trip to go see a tomb, he doubted anyone would have been stupid enough to try before. But up to three days ago he never had any doubts that TMS was an ideal society. *More controlled information?*

Now everything was different.

Sudden movement caught Joseph's eye. Five rock runners ripped by overhead. He had never seen them going so fast.

"They found my boy," he said, urging himself to have hope.

But hope was distant.

# CHAPTER THIRTY-ONE

Joey stared at Stan, his eyes burning. Whatever anger he felt for Michael or Ganyon was a bit of grit in the hinges compared to the rage he felt bubbling up now. But that quickly gave way to a rising hopelessness. *I wish I'd never found the tile.* But he had found it, and there was no changing that. And would it have mattered anyway? TMS didn't want miners who asked questions, or observed.

"Okay. Won't the long-range transport get here first?" Joey said, clawing for a small scrap of hope.

"I don't know."

"Well, what about the slave traders?"

"It's coded. I don't think they—"

"How could you do this to me?" Joey said.

"It's too dangerous out here. We'll be safe at TMS."

"But I don't want to go back."

"Why? You don't have to worry about anything. We take care of you."

"I should get to decide if I want that."

"None of us get to decide. I don't get to decide about being governor."

"Why can't you? Let's go to Mars."

"I never wanted to go," Stan said, looking Joey in the eye for the first time in a while. "At least, I don't think I did. I wanted my dad to come for me. I want him to miss me and eat dinner with me like your dad does."

"Is there even an Earth-Mars transport?"

"There is. But I don't know if they'll get the ELT signal."

Joey let out a short, bitter laugh. Stan really was taking his pet for a walk.

Joey stared unblinking for a long moment. His oxygen was down to 6.597%. Then 6.594%. He was losing air as if he were running. TMS was coming to rescue them. If he sat still maybe he would have enough air. Enough for what? *Enough to get me back to my pickaxe?*

He sat up and looked at the last asteroid, a long sliver of a crescent that dominated the sky. The rest of its massive form was blackness blotting out the stars beyond. The tomb was so close, yet unreachable.

If the tomb was even there. The rock could be as empty as the rest of the asteroids, with only subtleties of color for variety. But that wouldn't be enough for him now. Would it have ever been enough? Or was he fooling himself? *Unless the Earth-Mars transport gets here first, I guess I'll find out,* Joey thought sourly.

He fantasized about what life would be like if the Earth-Mars transport came and rescued them. As always, he didn't know enough about it to truly imagine. For all he knew they would give him back to TMS. If someone found his pickaxe, it would have been given back. So why would this be any different?

What if they did take him? Would they go back for his dad? Would TMS stop him from leaving? The thought of never seeing his dad again made his eyes well up with tears. But the idea of going back to mining was claustrophobic. It was death, maybe even worse.

Joey imagined living in the reffie village with his dad and Arabelle. It was a child's fantasy, easily connecting things that had no relation. Before meeting her he didn't even have the context for such a fantasy. But now the idea of living with the beautiful woman and his dad seemed so natural. She would love Joseph Senior's cooking, of course. Maybe they would live on Earth like his dad always dreamed. And they would taste a fresh apple.

The fantasy started to coalesce into a plan. He would get back to the village, recharge his suit, then sneak back into TMS and tell his dad everything. They would escape to the reffie village together.

He checked his oxygen again and his heart sank. There was maybe enough left for one more jump. And the first jump would be back to where the slave traders were. But what choice did he have?

He imagined the number of steps toward the edge of the rocky field they were on. How long had it been since he counted everything? How long since he felt the need to quiet his mind like that? The more he had wandered the asteroid cluster, the more letting his mind wander felt right. Life out here was terrifying and exciting, but filled with infinite branching possibilities. Life back on the colony was like the conveyors that carried ore into the processors. The ore went one way and only one way, and in the end the machines crushed it.

Joey had not noticed how blurry with tears his eyes were until they started to clear. And that's when he saw it. In the black of the unlit side of the last asteroid, a faint blue light shone. It was so faint he blinked and lost sight of it.

Joey looked at Stan. He wanted to tell someone and Stan was the only one there.

"Stan! Look!"

Stan turned to see where Joey pointed. Joey caught the blue light again just as it reached the edge of the asteroid and was carried out of view by the slow rotation of the massive rock.

"Did you see it?"

"Yes," Stan said with no joy.

"It's the tomb."

"It doesn't matter," Stan said, sounding bleak. "We don't have enough power or oxygen to go there."

Minutes later, a single broken spire of galaxite crested the edge of the asteroid. The sun lit it as if fire raged inside. Then, as it crossed slowly into the dark, the column dimmed, and he saw the blue light again. He started counting.

"Did you hear me?" Stan said. "We'd die if—"

"Shut up," Joey snapped and kept counting, with his eye fixed unblinking on that blue glow. It took a count to six hundred and twenty for the blue light to vanish again. A little over ten minutes. Joey estimated if he jumped in six minutes he should land near that faint blue glow. He wasn't smart like Stan, but all the jumps in the past two days gave him confidence.

His oxygen was at 5.745% now. He counted. Stan said something to him but he didn't listen. At two hundred and eighty he got up, stomped his heel, and ran.

"Joey!" Stan yelled behind him.

Joey ignored him. He had to jump by the time his count hit three hundred and sixty. He leapt upward and flew toward the blackness in front of him. Whatever happened now, he was committed. Whatever happened, even the worst he could imagine, was better than the thought of being back at TMS. Even if TMS had nice masters.

"I am Olly," Joey said to himself. *I'm not just an Olly, I am THE Olly. Everything I am doing will cost me dearly.*

# CHAPTER THIRTY-TWO

The micro thrusters came alive as Joey's suit picked up the gravity of RN-4u, the last asteroid in the cluster. It was the shortest jump he had made. He was flipped around and there was no hanging in the dead zone.

He would fall wherever the gravity took him. Until this jump, that was always toward the daylight side of an asteroid. Was that luck? Was it Stan's planning? That hardly mattered now. This time he fell toward blackness. The crescent edge of RN-4u was his only reference for speed. All seemed normal.

And then he fell faster.

*"Thrusters Critical. Thrusters Critical."* The suit's warning systems burst to life. The micro thrusters sputtered out unevenly, causing him to tumble very, very slowly.

Joey looked for the blue light. He found it. Fixated on it. It was his only judge of distance and speed. His slow tumble spun him around, and he lost sight of the light again.

The thrusters stuttered back to life before dying.

They stabilized him so he was a least upright. But still corkscrewing.

"*Thrusters Fail! Thrusters Fail!*"

With nothing to guide him, and no micro thrusters to slow his decent, Joey prepared for the landing as best he could. He was in total blackness save for that dim blue light, and the thin crescent of sunlight on the asteroid's edge. Both spun slowly in his vision. The low gravity was the only hope that his legs wouldn't shatter.

His feet slammed into brittle flaking rocks. Rocks and dust exploded around him. His legs gave out and his body twisted into a tumble. He rolled and bounced off the surface, kicking up more rocks and soil, and in the low gravity, he started to float off the ground. He managed to grab hold of a jagged rock. Even with the tough padding of the AGLS gloves, the edge dug into his hands. His momentum threw his legs over the rock in a wide arc, and he slammed down on the other side. Every muscle and every joint hurt, but he held on. And he did not break his glass dome. Had he slipped he might not have come down again for an hour.

"*Oxygen Critical. Oxygen Critical.*"

Joey checked the readout on his forearm. He silenced the alarm without checking the levels. All the numbers were red and that told him enough. There wasn't much time. He had to get moving before Stan's beacon brought TMS. If he was going to be dragged back, he was going to see the tomb.

He looked around for the light and found it. It was mounted on a column about waist height. Dim light caught the broken galaxite columns beyond.

Joey looked for Stan. He could just make out a white speck on the other asteroid.

"Stan!" Joey yelled as loud as he could, hoping ShortComs would carry that far. "I made it."

A brief blast of static came back, stinging his ears and then going silent.

On the daylight side of all but the darkest asteroids, stars were rarely visible. But here on the night side, the Milky Way was dazzling. Joey wanted to sit down and rest, and stare at the beauty of it all. But he could do that later. Later, when he was back to being a slave with nice masters.

He fixed his gaze on the blue light again. The dimming work lights in his suit would help him avoid rocks directly in front of him and not much else. He took a step, stumbled, and found himself floating across the ground. Every part of the ground he touched broke away in pieces. Without the micro thruster his weight was not enough to press him to the surface. He was forced to cling to the rocks and pull himself along. He repeatedly checked his bearings against the blue light.

At last, he reached the rock column and realized it was a statue, damaged into a vague humanlike form that was broken off above the hands holding the light. Joey shielded his eyes as the asteroid's rotation carried him into the sunlight. The galaxite spire lit up like a giant version of light tubes in Joey's kitchen. The blue light was swallowed in the brightness. The fast rotation of RN-4u was dizzying. Before long, he was back in blackness.

The source of the light was set in a bowl-shaped stone held by the hands of the statue. It was a thick disk of glass about the size of his splayed fingers. The glow came from deep under the smooth glassy surface. This connection to the tile comforted him.

His muscles were tight, filled with small knifelike knots. He felt as if a hot liquid spread deep inside his knee, and it was left with a dull persistent ache. But his mind, which had been growing tired, was now electrified.

With no other plan, Joey hovered his hand over the blue light. It grew more intense, as the dots on the tile had. And the same static scratched through the Angel's speakers. He placed his hand on the glassy surface. Through the glove, a slight vibration hummed, and the static in his ears grew. He pressed down on the interface, and the disk sank into the bowl.

The ground shook.

As he was carried into the darkness again, great chunks of galaxite slid off the mound in front of him. A massive round door thrust straight up from the sloped side of the mound, sending rocks and dust flying. Joey sheltered behind the broken statue.

Dim light spilled out from the gaps around the door. When the entire bulk of it was clear of the rocks, the door swung out, throwing any remaining rocks high into the sky. The circular hole in the low mound beckoned him. And Joey answered its call.

As he got closer, a brilliant light blasted out of the doorway, spearing a hundred-meter-tall shaft of light through the dust. Joey shielded his eyes and stumbled backward.

He caught his balance and stepped up to the entrance. The blast of light subsided, leaving only a pale glow spilling from the hole. A staircase curved away below him. The steps and the walls alike were a milky, translucent stone, like a pale jade. There were no seams; the edges of each step flowed into the curved walls of the tunnel. Like the surface of tile, there were subtle circular scratches on every surface. They could have been designs, or tool marks.

Joey turned the AGLS lights off. He didn't check the levels of his life support. Whatever happened from here, the only thing he had left was to see.

# CHAPTER THIRTY-THREE

J oey descended the stairs, floating as much as stepping. At the base of the steps it was dark. Only the light of the tunnel gave him any hint there was more down there. But as he took the final step onto the floor, warm light bloomed.

A bulbous block of galaxite dominated the oval room. It was longer than a man, and wider, and about a meter tall. Just like Stan had said, it was a human-shaped box, lying on its back. The soft, glowing jade of the floor flowed seamlessly into the sarcophagus and lit it from below. Inside its glassy depth there was a long dark shape. The smokey glass distorted the shape beyond description.

*A person wrapped in blankets?*

He stared for a long time, nervous that this was all a dream and if he took the wrong step the dream would melt away and he'd wake back at TMS. The room plunged back into darkness.

Joey turned on the AGLS work lights and float-walked to look closer. A deep crack divided the sarcophagus and continued across the floor.

The room lit up again. The light poured out of a galaxite column set in the wall beyond the sarcophagus. He realized it was the base of the spire he had seen outside, and it carried the light of the sun down into the tomb.

The light picked out intricate carvings of figures in the back wall. The forms of them were unidentifiable—human, but also not. Joey had sometimes drawn people in weird, exaggerated ways. Maybe these figures were the same. He hoped not. He wanted them to be some alien race who came from a distance and time beyond imagination.

Joey hadn't even realized how cold he had been until it started to drain away. He was warm now, and a sense of calm spread through him as he got closer to the sarcophagus. This galaxite was free of pits or abrasions, or even a coating of dust. It was clean and beautiful and Joey's gaze sank into it as if he were falling.

He shook that feeling out of his head and ran his hand along the hulking shape. The form inside was definitely big enough to be a man.

He felt along the crack. He could just fit two gloved fingers inside. Deep below the thick glass something caught the light. There was something like skin, deep brown, wrinkled, and dried to a dull gloss. It was wrapped in a golden-yellow fabric. No matter how he positioned himself, he could not see more than that sliver. He pushed on one side of the crack and then the other, but neither would budge.

The light sank away again and Joey waited out the darkness. TMS would be there soon. He hated the idea of going back but for some reason couldn't be upset about it now.

When the light returned, he pulled out his notebook and drew everything. With a contented smile, he drew until he ran out of pages in the book. Then he drew over the old drawing of equipment. He drew until the room dimmed again.

Whether he would be rescued or not, and whether he had to go back to being a slave or not, his purpose, however trivial and futile it seemed in the scheme of the cosmos, had been to see this tomb.

And if rescue didn't come, maybe in another thousand years he would be discovered, frozen. His drawings would be found. Would they know he was an escaped slave? Would they think he was like Stan, out on a trip to make his dad upset, and meeting an unfortunate end? Would they make up some other story in their minds?

Joey saved one blank spot in the notebook. He drew the sliver of skin and the surrounding crack in great detail. Before he could finish the drawing, the light faded again.

When the light returned, it continued to get brighter and brighter until Joey shut his eyes. It got brighter still until his eyelids weren't enough to shut out the light. Joey stumbled back. His eyes shot open on their own. The light coalesced into a ball of golden-white fire hovering above the sarcophagus. It flowed outward in smokey tendrils and enveloped him and carried him backward. Carried him up through the tunnel and out of the tomb.

It carried him across the gulf between RN-4u

and RN-4i, and he drifted toward Stan, who still sat there with his head on his knees. His friend looked up, squinting against the bright glow. He drifted past the slave traders, still searching for them around the galaxite wall. And as the light passed overhead, they ran for cover. He drifted all the way back to the refugee village. He was running up the row of cargo boxes and apartments now. Running to the one that he knew was his. He shouted with joy as he saw his dad come out of the door with his arm around the beautiful Arabelle.

And Joey jumped into their arms.

*Liberty, the greatest of all earthly blessings—give us that precious jewel and you may take everything else!*

—Patrick Henry

# A TOMB
### IN THE
# ROCKS

If you enjoyed A Tomb in the Rocks, please consider adding
a review to your favorite bookseller's website. You can find
links to them by scanning the QR Code below. I would be
grateful if you could spare five minutes to do that. It need
only be a line or two and it makes a massive difference.

**AlexGuyBooks.com**

Alexander Guy is the Science Fiction and Fantasy pen name of Chris Neuhahn, animation producer, director, writer and Emmy winner. He lives in Los Angeles with his beautiful wife who he calls The Rabbit.

You can sign up for Alex's newsletter on his website to get updates on future books. Including the upcoming Urban Fantasy series where Classic fairytales get a hardboiled detective twist in Fairyland Murders. In an alternate post war America, you'll follow a Clurichaun detective as he tracks your favorite fairytales to their logical and gruesome conclusions.

**AlexGuyBooks.com**